The sound of Charlie cooing made Chuck's heart skip several beats.

Chuck glanced at PJ standing with her back to him. "How was it? Your pregnancy, the delivery? I want to know."

"I did fine."

"I would have been there..

"I know you would have. If

"Why didn't you tell me?" C the crook of his arm and s face.

"Your focus needed to be on staying alive," PJ said. "What was the point in telling you?"

His anger stirred again. "The point is, I'm Charlie's father."

"And if there had been complications, what could you have done from Afghanistan?"

Chuck sighed. "Nothing."

A long silence stretched between them.

"I won't try to keep you from seeing Charlie," PJ said.

Chuck liked the strong, determined woman she'd grown into in the year he'd been away, and found himself even more attracted to her than before. But he wasn't as sure about where they stood, or if he trusted her with his heart.

you could have.

uck tipped Charlie into
ared down into her little

BODYGUARD UNDER FIRE

—

ELLE JAMES

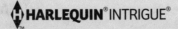

This book is dedicated to my father who sacrificed a lot for his country and his family. He's the rock in my life and I love him so much.

Recycling programs for this product may not exist in your area.

ISBN-13: 978-0-373-74767-2

BODYGUARD UNDER FIRE

Copyright © 2013 by Mary Jernigan

Printed in U.S.A.

www.Harlequin.com

ABOUT THE AUTHOR

A Golden Heart Award winner for Best Paranormal Romance in 2004, Elle James started writing when her sister issued a Y2K challenge to write a romance novel. She has managed a full-time job and raised three wonderful children, and she and her husband even tried their hands at ranching exotic birds (ostriches, emus and rheas) in the Texas Hill Country. Ask her, and she'll tell you what it's like to go toe-to-toe with an angry 350-pound bird! After leaving her successful career in information technology management, Elle is now pursuing her writing full-time. Elle loves to hear from fans. You can contact her at ellejames@earthlink.net or visit her website at www.ellejames.com.

Books by Elle James

CAST OF CHARACTERS

Chuck Bolton—Wounded soldier returning to Wild Oak Canyon to join Hank Derringer's team, Covert Cowboys, Inc.

PJ Franks—Waitress at Cara Jo's diner, going to night school to make a better life for her and her baby girl.

Cara Jo Smithson—Owner of Cara Jo's Diner, new manager of the Wild Oak Canyon Resort, and PJ's friend.

Hank Derringer—Billionaire willing to take the fight for justice into his own hands by setting up CCI— Covert Cowboys, Inc.

Emilio Montalvo—Wealthy Mexican investor with possible connections to a ruthless drug cartel.

Ricardo Iglesias—Mexican guest at the Wild Oak Canyon Resort with an interest in getting to know PJ.

Ross Felton—Hardware store owner's surly grandson with a knack for all things to do with computers.

Dana Perkins—Woman who looks after PJ's baby while PJ works and goes to school.

Brandon Pendley—Hank Derringer's computer guru, responsible for setting up the Raging Bull Ranch security system.

Alana Rodriguez—A woman Hank Derringer helped escape from a bad situation twenty-five years ago.

Chapter One

Chuck Bolton walked to the edge of town, working the kinks out of his bum leg, his limp more pronounced after his two-hour ride on one of the resort nags, housed in the old-fashioned livery stable.

He hadn't had much call to ride in the military, spending most of his time on foot or in an armorplated vehicle, patrolling the villages and Taliban-riddled hillsides of Afghanistan.

He'd still be there had he not turned all Rambo and gone off the deep end. Some called him a hero. His commander called him an idiot for risking his life. But other than ending his military career, he couldn't regret his vigilante justice on the Taliban stronghold he'd leveled to the ground single-handed.

After what they'd done to that kid...

Chuck shook his head to clear the images. That was the past. Wild Oak Canyon and Covert Cowboys, Inc. were his future.

On the edge of town, looking south, he drew in a deep breath of hot, dry air and let it out. Not many understood the lure of this parched desert or chose to live here. Outsiders didn't last long, not with miles and miles of flat, unchanging terrain, with the Davis Mountains rising in the distance, appearing closer than they actually were.

Hell, Chuck might not have come back had he not been invited to join CCI, the secret organization billionaire ranch owner Hank Derringer had started recently. Wild Oak Canyon held too many memories, both good and bad.

Everywhere he turned he ran into mental images of PJ.

PJ riding a horse across the desert landscape, PJ smiling up at him from their favorite swimming hole, begging him to join her, PJ telling him she'd love him forever…

Forever had been all too short. She'd begged him not to volunteer for the rotation to Afghanistan, wanting him to wait until his unit was called up, giving them a little more time together before he was put into harm's way. His Army National Guard unit hadn't been due for rotation for another twelve months when a call went out for volunteers.

Chuck had insisted on going, telling her duty called and he had to go.

They'd argued, Chuck had said things he wished he hadn't, his temper getting the better of him. Looking back, he could see that PJ had been scared, afraid of losing him. And he'd pushed her away so effectively she'd ended their engagement, throwing the ring in his face shortly before he'd left for predeployment training at Fort Hood.

God, he'd been so stubborn. If only he'd said he was sorry, they might be married by now. He wouldn't be wandering the streets of Wild Oak Canyon in search of what he'd lost.

Yeah, and if wishes were horses, he probably would have been bucked off on his butt anyway.

Bottom line was that he was back. He hadn't had the nerve to look up PJ yet and wouldn't. That didn't stop his gaze from searching every face passing by on foot or in cars and trucks.

So far, he hadn't seen her. For all he knew, she might not be here at all. The last correspondence he'd had from her was a letter asking where she could send the things he'd accumulated at her house. The address had been the same house she'd lived in with her mother in Wild Oak Canyon, but that had been a year ago. A lot changed in a year. He'd driven by that address when he'd gotten to town. A Hispanic family with two small children lived there now.

Chuck performed a clumsy about-face and headed back to the Wild Oak Canyon Resort staff quarters, his temporary lodging for the assignment Hank had given him.

His cover was as a handyman, fixing things around the resort and Cara Jo's Diner, adjacent to the resort compound. Cara Jo Smithson, the most recent owner of the diner and the new property manager for the resort, would give him the particulars about the real assignment. He was to be a bodyguard for one of her employees. No one was to know that but Hank, Cara Jo and Chuck. Not even the employee. What was so special about that person that he needed protecting? Chuck wouldn't know until Cara Jo returned from her supply run to Fort Stockton. She'd fill him in with all the particulars of the case then.

Hank had given him a key to one of the rooms in the resort staff quarters. The room was at the back of the resort closest to the diner. From what he could tell, there were only two staff rooms in this wing of the resort, and they shared a bathroom down the hall.

After settling his duffle bag in the room, Chuck had examined the exterior of the diner and the resort compound. Wild Oak Canyon's Main Street and the resort had a quaint Wild West theme with weathered-wood storefronts, an old-style barbershop, a general store and a saloon with a hitching post out front. Cara Jo's Diner was just like the rest of the town, only some of the weathered wood needed repair before someone got hurt or the building suffered further damage from wind and the elements.

Chuck noted weatherworn boards peeling up on the porch, along with a splintered railing and loose shingles on the roof. One of the eaves had rotted through and would need replacing. As soon as he had sufficient supplies, he'd go to work on those

little fix-it items. They wouldn't keep him busy for
long. He hoped there was more work to be done on
the inside of the resort or maybe the old livery stable. He preferred working outside, especially around
animals. They weren't as judgmental as people.

Until he had the supplies and his marching orders, he was at loose ends with energy to burn.
Thus the ride, followed by a walk to the end of
town and back.

Temperatures hovered close to ninety, even after
the sun set and the stars came out to fill the night
sky with their brilliance.

Chuck headed to the resort. The back door to the
office remained locked, no light inside indicating
Ms. Smithson's return.

Sweaty and smelling of horse, Chuck decided
on a shower before his meeting with the boss lady
and clumped up the stairs to his room. After gathering soap, shaving gear and a towel, he slipped off
his boots and socks and headed down the hallway.

A noise in the room beside his had him leaning
in toward the door. A baby cried, and a woman's
voice talked softly, soothing it.

Chuck knocked on the door. Was Ms. Smithson
younger than he'd thought? Did she have a baby?

After a long moment the door opened to a slim,
pale-skinned young woman with dark hair piled in
a messy bun on the back of her head. She clutched a
baby in her arms, balancing a bottle under her chin
as she juggled the door handle and tried to look up

at him. "Yes?" she managed without dropping her chin-hold on the bottle.

"Are you Cara Jo?" Chuck asked.

She let go of the door and gripped the bottle, holding it for the baby to feed. "Oh, no, I'm Dana. Cara Jo is the owner of the diner. She lives above it."

"Sorry, I'm supposed to meet with her about a job. I'm your new neighbor." He jerked his head to the left toward his apartment door.

"Oh, you must be the handyman." She balanced the bottle with her chin again and held out her hand. "I'm Dana. Cara Jo should be back any minute. She left early this morning for Fort Stockton to get supplies for the resort and diner. They said they'd be back by nine tonight. It's almost nine now."

"I'm Chuck Bolton. Nice to meet you, Dana."

"Good to have a handyman around again. My, but you are very tall."

He smiled. He got that a lot. At six feet five inches, he tended to be taller than most men. "I can see that you're busy. I won't bother you." He glanced down at the baby, a bubbly, milky smile spreading across her face. Her brown hair curled across her forehead, and the big brown eyes were in sharp contrast to Dana's cornflower-blue eyes. "Cute baby."

Dana smiled down at the child in her arms. "Hear that, Charlie? He thinks you're cute. Me, too, my sweet little baby girl."

"I guess I'll be seeing you around." He chucked

the baby under the chin and she reached out, snagging his finger in her tight little grip. "A little tiger, aren't you?" He smiled down at the baby, his heart squeezing in his chest. He'd had dreams of him and PJ raising a family together. A strapping brown-haired, brown-eyed boy like him, and an angelic blond-haired, green-eyed girl the spitting image of her mother.

The phone rang in the apartment behind Dana. "Excuse me. Nice to meet you."

Chuck turned away as Dana shut the door.

Yet another reminder of PJ and the family they should have had. He needed to get over her and get on with his life.

It just wasn't that easy.

CARA JO DROVE the truck behind the resort and backed up close to the rear entrance of the diner. "I don't know about you, but I'm past exhausted. What say we leave most of this stuff in the back until tomorrow, when we can get some help unloading?"

Peggy Jane Franks dropped down out of the truck and stretched. "Agreed. We can grab the perishables and store them in the walk-in refrigerator and call it a night. I want to see Charlie."

Mentioning her daughter made PJ smile. An entire day away from her baby made PJ miss her so much it hurt.

Cara Jo dropped the tailgate and slid the ice chests full of everything from butter to frozen yogurt to the edge. The normal delivery truck had broken down in Fort Stockton, and they were running low on supplies. Otherwise they wouldn't have made the long drive themselves.

Once they had the food stored in the freezer and refrigerator in the restaurant, PJ hurried up the back stairs of the resort, hoping to catch Charlie awake. They'd arrived later than she'd expected, and Dana would be tired and ready to go home.

PJ fit her key in the lock of her small apartment and pushed the door open. "Hey, Dana, I'm home."

Dana looked up from bending over the crib, situated just inside the bedroom door. "Oh, it's you."

PJ laughed. "Yeah, it's me. Expecting anyone else?"

Dana smiled. "No, no. I just met the new handyman Cara Jo hired out in the hallway a few minutes ago. I thought maybe he got lost on his way back to his room."

"How's my sweet Charlie?" PJ crossed the room, anxious to hold her daughter.

Dana lifted the baby out of her crib and handed her to PJ. "She was just about to nod off, but when she heard your voice, her eyes popped wide open."

PJ smiled down at Charlie and hugged her against her. "Hey, sweetie, did you miss your mommy?"

Charlie cooed up at her, a toothless smile spreading across her face.

"Of course she did. The sun rises and sets on you,

in Miss Charlie's eyes." Dana stared down at the child in PJ's arms. "You're so very lucky."

"I know." PJ kissed Charlie's cheek. Charlie was a perfect baby, full of joy and so easy to take care of. Everyone loved her.

Dana touched PJ's shoulder. "I gotta run. Tommy will be yowling for dinner."

PJ glanced up. "This late?"

"You'd think the man didn't know what a microwave oven was. I bet he didn't bother to get the plate I left for him this morning out of the refrigerator." Dana laughed and smiled at Charlie. "She was an angel."

"Ha. I'll bet she wore you out."

"Not at all. I didn't mind watching her a bit." Dana's eyes glistened.

"You're a natural, Dana. Have you talked to the doctor again? Is there anything you can do?"

"It's in God's hands." Dana smiled through unshed tears. "Two miscarriages must be a sign it isn't meant to be."

"Don't talk like that. It'll happen when you least expect it." As it had happened for PJ.

"I'm not getting my hopes up. Been there too many times and cried buckets of tears." Dana hugged PJ. "Take care of my baby. I think I could love her as much as you do." Dana left, closing the door behind her.

Alone at last with Charlie, PJ dropped into her

rocking chair. It wouldn't take much for Charlie to fall asleep, but PJ wanted to hold her a little longer. The sweet scent of baby shampoo and powder filled her senses and gave her a feeling of home.

After a few minutes Charlie slept, her mouth working a sucking motion, the fingers of one hand bunched into a tiny fist. She looked so much like her father—brown hair, brown eyes and ready for a fight.

PJ chuckled, her laughter catching on a sob. She missed Chuck so much she thought she might die sometimes. If not for sweet Charlie, she might have lost the will to live altogether.

Still wearing the clothes she'd traveled in, PJ felt wrinkled, covered in road grime and in need of a shower to wash away the stress of the long drive.

She laid Charlie in her crib and gathered clothing, a bathrobe and toiletries. Switching on the baby monitor, PJ tucked the receiver in her pocket and headed for the door to her suite. She exited and turned to lock the door behind her.

The bathroom was between her suite and the only other staff apartment in this section of the building. When she opened the door, a waft of warm, moist air and a scent she could never forget enveloped her.

Someone had used the shower. Must be the new handyman Cara Jo had spoken of on their trip to Fort Stockton.

PJ's stomach clenched, and her fingers tightened

around the doorknob. The new guy would have to use the same soap Chuck had, and damned if he didn't also use the same cologne. As tired as she was, PJ could barely hold it together as the aromas washed over her, bringing back memories best left in the back of her mind.

She had to have a shower and didn't have another option close enough to her room that the monitor would carry to, so PJ closed the door behind her. Her hands shook as she set the monitor on the sink and turned it up loud enough that she could hear it over the water's spray.

With quick, efficient movements, she flung off her clothes and stepped beneath the cool spray. She was fast about her showers, concerned about leaving Charlie alone too long.

After a quick shampoo and rinse, she ducked her head around the curtain and listened to the monitor. A reassuring staticky silence was all she heard. As she closed the shower curtain, a different sound carried over the speaker.

Click.

PJ strained her ears.

Click.

She shut off the water and listened more intently.

Click.

Then a sharp sound, like something falling, echoed through the monitor.

What the hell?

PJ pulled on her pajama bottoms and top, grabbed her key and flung the bathroom door open.

The door to her apartment stood open.

PJ's heart slammed to a halt and then kicked into high gear. She had been careful to close and lock the door when she'd left. As she stared into her dark apartment, fear rooted her to the floor for only a moment.

Her baby daughter was in that room. Cold dread filled her and she shot forward, ready to take down anyone who threatened to harm…

"Charlie," she said and launched forward.

When she stepped through the open door, a dark figure wearing a black ski mask grabbed her and flung her inside.

PJ screamed and scurried backward and then turned to run. She made it only one step before a hand latched onto her hair and yanked her backward.

PJ screamed again, her cry cut off by a large gloved hand clamping down over her mouth. She bit into it, her teeth barely making a dent in the thick leather glove.

She kicked and slammed her elbow into his gut, but he wouldn't release her hair, the pressure on the roots pulling her skin tight over her forehead, pain radiating through her scalp.

All PJ could think about was Charlie. She had to protect her from this madman. Giving up was not an option. She stomped hard on the man's instep and he yelled, let go of her hair and backhanded her so hard she flew across the room, tripped over the couch and fell against an end table. The lamp on the table teetered. PJ grabbed it and swung it at the man's head. The ceramic base hit him in the ear and shattered.

He grabbed the electric cord, ripped it from the wall and wrapped it around PJ's neck, pulling it tight.

PJ's fingers fumbled for the cord, panic setting in as her vision blurred, her air cut off. No. She couldn't die. Charlie needed her. She kicked and twisted, managing only to tighten the cord around her throat. It couldn't end this way. She wouldn't let it happen.

The man lifted her to her feet and dragged her backward toward the door.

PJ's feet flailed beneath her, her strength fading with lack of oxygen. She focused on the crib in the bedroom and gave new effort to saving her own skin. With all the force she could muster, she brought her heel up hard between her attacker's legs.

The man grunted and slumped forward, jerking harder on the cord around her neck.

Her world faded and her strength drained. She couldn't give up.

A loud crash sounded behind her as her apartment door slammed inward, bouncing off the wall. PJ heard it but couldn't see who'd entered. All she could hope was that the cavalry had arrived to save her and Charlie.

Her attacker jerked, releasing his hold on the cord around PJ's neck.

PJ pitched forward to her hands and knees and crawled away, dragging in huge gulps of air. When she turned, the man in black sailed through the air toward her.

She threw herself to the side in time to avoid the collision.

The man hit the ground hard, rolled to his feet and dived for the sliding glass door leading onto the balcony, slamming it open.

Her savior charged after him, naked to the waist, his body glistening with droplets of water.

It all happened so fast, PJ didn't see his face, only his hulking size and rippling, well-toned muscles flashing past.

The attacker in black launched himself over the balcony and dropped to the pavement below, disappearing out of sight. The bare-chested man braced his hands on the rail, his muscles bunched, ready to follow, and then he hesitated.

He stood with his back to PJ for a long, agonizing moment. Would he jump?

PJ prayed he wouldn't. She didn't wish for her hero to be hurt in the fall. At long last, he turned to face her.

Ready to thank her rescuer, PJ's breath left her lungs in a rush.

"Oh, dear God." She pressed her fist to her mouth, her eyes filling with tears, all her hopes and fears of ever seeing this man again wrapped up in one word. "Chuck."

PJ's world faded into black.

Chapter Two

Chuck's instinct had been to leap over the railing and chase after the black-clad attacker and pummel him into a bloody pulp for terrorizing his neighbor. As he'd bent his knees to do just that, pain ripped through his bad leg, reminding him that he couldn't and shouldn't drop fifteen feet to the ground if he wanted to keep the leg to walk on. Even if his leg survived the landing, he wasn't up to running full speed yet.

Defeat rode heavily on his shoulders as he swung back to the woman pulling herself to her feet in the doorway.

She shifted in the shadows, and the overhead light illuminated her sandy-blond hair.

Chuck's heart burst into a gallop, pounding against his ribs. The throbbing pain in his bum leg faded to the back of his mind as joy filled him at the sight of her. He stepped forward.

Her eyes widened and she stepped back. "Chuck?"

"PJ?"

And she crumpled to the floor.

Had he been able, he'd have caught her before she landed. His injury-induced limitations hampered him in his rush to get to her.

Chuck gathered PJ into his arms, his heart plummeting to the bottom of his belly at her reaction when she'd recognized him.

The entire time he'd been in the oppressive heat and constant dust of Afghanistan, he'd pictured her coming to greet him upon his return, arms wide, a smile of happiness lighting her eyes. In the back of his mind, he'd known it was only a dream.

The stark reality of her standing in front of him, her hands clenching and unclenching at her sides, her face blanching before she passed out, shattered those silly dreams.

She was no happier to see him return than she had been to see him leave. Shock best described her response.

Crushed, Chuck held her, cherishing every second he could feel her against him. He examined the bruising around her throat, anger firming his spine, pushing aside his deep disappointment. Who would attack a lone woman like that? Why would anyone want to hurt PJ? Since he hadn't spoken to Cara Jo yet, he couldn't be certain, but he'd bet his right arm that this was the employee Hank wanted protected.

Chuck had walked into this assignment blind. Hank had assured him Cara Jo would fill him in on what his duties were and, when he had met the employee, he could go to Hank with any unanswered questions.

Chuck had a few, and the sooner he got his answers the better.

After only a moment, PJ's face stirred against his chest and her eyes blinked open. "Chuck, what are you doing here? I thought you were still in Afghanistan." She pushed to a sitting position.

His lips tightened. Had he not been a loose cannon and acted on his own, he would still be in Afghanistan for another two months, fighting with his unit. Instead he'd gotten himself shot in the leg and medically discharged out of the army. "The army didn't need me there after all." It wasn't a lie. The army didn't need broken soldiers.

"Oh." Her gaze traveled across his naked chest, her cheeks reddening. "Why are you half-naked?"

His lips twisted into a wry grin. "I just hired on with the resort as the handyman. I live down the hall." He frowned. "Why are you in this apartment? I met a woman here a little while ago named Donna or Dana or something like that. She had a baby."

The baby whimpered from inside the bedroom as if emphasizing Chuck's question.

PJ's face paled at the sound, her gaze shifting to the crib against the wall inside the next room. She pushed his hands aside and rose to her feet. "I live here."

Chuck straightened, heat rushing up his neck into

his head. Like a zombie, he trudged toward the bedroom, his fists tightening, a sharp pain pinching his chest. "Then who is…?" In the dimly lit room, Chuck peered down at the baby with a tuft of silky dark hair, and his world crashed in around him as he remembered what Dana had said. "She called her Charlie," he said, his voice raspy, uneven.

PJ entered the room, switched on a lamp and leaned over the crib, running her fingers over the baby's face and body. "She seems to be okay."

The baby slept through PJ's touch, a soft smile curling her little lips, as if she knew she was safe and in good hands. "I named her after her father," PJ whispered.

"Charlie." Chuck's fingers curled around the crib rail so tightly his knuckles turned white. "Why didn't you tell me?"

PJ sighed. "You were in Afghanistan. What could you have done? From what I know, the army doesn't grant leave from a war zone just so a man can be there when his baby is born, unless under dire circumstances."

"I had a right to know." His words came out sharper than he intended, but hell, what did she expect? A man didn't learn he had a daughter every day. The news had his belly flipping into knots.

"So, now you know." PJ brushed her fingers over her daughter's hair and stepped back. "You have a right to be angry. But I didn't know what else to do. We didn't part on the best of terms."

A muscle jerked in his jaw, and he had to breathe several calming breaths before he could speak again. "Call the police."

PJ passed through the small living area and into the kitchen. Her purse lay strewn across the counter. She dug her cell phone out of a side pocket, hit three buttons and then walked back to the threshold of the bedroom, her gaze on the baby in the crib. "This is PJ Franks at the Wild Oak Canyon Resort. I need to report an intruder attack."

When she'd given details to the dispatcher, she hung up and glanced at Chuck. "They're sending a unit."

Chuck straightened and crossed to her, his fingers reaching out to touch her throat. "We should have asked for an ambulance, as well."

Her eyes filled, but she shook her head. "No. I'm fine." She raised her hands to the bruising around her neck and gulped. "I was so afraid." PJ's head dipped.

Chuck pulled her into his arms. No matter how mad he was, he never could stand to see PJ cry, and after seeing a man choking the life out of her, now was no different. "He's gone."

"Yeah, but why was he here in the first place?" She pushed away from him and wandered back into the living room.

Chuck followed. "Is anything missing?"

She checked her purse, thumbing through her wallet. What few bills she'd had were still there, along with her credit card and identification. "The items were scattered across the counter, but nothing seems to be missing."

"What about the rest of the apartment?"

"I don't have anything of value. Just a few keepsakes and used furniture. As a waitress, I can't afford much." PJ continued around the room, her fingers skimming across the top of the old couch Cara Jo had given her. She ducked into her bedroom and came back out, holding a photo frame, a frown denting her forehead. "This photo is the only thing out of place. It was standing on my nightstand when I left for my shower. I just found it lying on its face."

"The intruder could have knocked it over." Chuck reached for the frame.

PJ handed it over. "It's a picture of me and my birth mother."

A woman looking remarkably like PJ held a child in her arms and was smiling for the photographer. Her eyes were shadowed, but the love for her little girl was clear in her expression.

"She died when you were little, didn't she?"

PJ nodded. "I was six. My adoptive mother, Terri Franks, pretty much raised me. We moved to Wild Oak Canyon before I started high school."

Chuck remembered the pretty young PJ hanging out around the stables, talking to the horses. She'd been more comfortable with the animals than with people.

A knock on the door was followed by a man's

voice. "PJ Franks? Sheriff's Deputy Johnny Owen. You called?"

PJ hurried to open the door for the officer.

He took her statement, in which she described the attacker, what he wore and which direction he'd gone.

Chuck searched the apartment, analyzing everything he saw for clues as to who had broken into PJ's apartment and why. All the while he fought to process the miracle of the baby in the next room. His child.

When Owen finished with PJ, the deputy asked Chuck a few questions and then tucked the pad of paper into his pocket and sighed. "Since the man was wearing gloves, I don't see a need to dust for prints. I'll have a look around outside to see if there are any footprints on the ground, but—"

"It's been dry, and the chance of a footprint showing up is slim to none," Chuck finished. "Thanks for trying."

After the deputy left, Chuck made a round of the apartment, checking the windows and sliding glass door locks.

When he'd deemed them secure, he met PJ at her open apartment door.

"It's getting late," she said. "I need to get some sleep before I hit the day shift at the diner."

"Will you be all right?" Chuck stepped into the door frame and gripped PJ's arms, his gaze capturing hers.

"I'll be fine." The shadows beneath her eyes spoke of her exhaustion and the lingering fear.

Fine, humph. Chuck wanted to hold her so badly, it hurt to drop his grip from her arms and walk out into the hallway. "If you need me…"

"You're just a yell away." She gave him a half smile.

Chuck nodded toward the interior of her apartment. "She's beautiful."

PJ's face reddened, and she nodded. "We'll discuss Charlie tomorrow."

"Yes, we will." Now that Chuck knew he had a daughter, he was determined to be a part of her life, whether PJ wanted him in *her* life or not.

PJ closed the door behind him.

Chuck waited until he heard the click of the lock being engaged. Then he hurried down the hallway to his room, grabbed a sleeping bag and a pillow and returned to bed down in front of PJ's door. As he stretched out on the floor and worked the kink out of his leg, he reminded himself that it beat sleeping in a foxhole. And he refused to let anything happen to PJ and his precious baby daughter, Charlie.

Once he was settled, he grabbed his cell phone and hit the speed dial number for Hank Derringer.

The older man answered on the third ring. "Derringer," he said, his voice scratchy and slurred with sleep.

"Hank, Chuck here. Tell me my assignment was just some sick joke on your part."

Hank sighed. "I take it you met PJ?"

"I did. You didn't tell me I'd be protecting my ex-fiancée."

"If I had, would you have taken the job?"

Chuck wanted to tell the man he would have, but truth was, he probably would have told Hank where to go with his job and assignment. "No."

"And now?" Hank asked.

With a sigh, Chuck answered. "You know damn well I can't walk away."

"I take it you met your daughter, Charlie?"

Chuck swallowed the lump forming in his throat. "Yes."

"Beautiful baby girl, isn't she?" Hank chuckled. "Looks like her father."

"How did you know?" Chuck asked.

"Let's just say I make it my business to know as much as I can about the people I hire. And I have a special interest in PJ that I won't go into at this time."

"Now that I'm here and know who I'm supposed to protect, maybe you can tell me why someone tried to kill PJ tonight."

AFTER PJ LOCKED the door behind Chuck, she'd leaned her head against the cool, wooden panel, telling herself to breathe.

Chuck still had too much of a hold on her, even after almost a year's separation. She thought pushing him out of her life had been the best decision at the time. Now she wasn't quite as convinced. Breaking their engagement had been only a part of it.

Even if Chuck hadn't insisted on volunteering, PJ suspected she'd have found another way to push him away. They'd gotten too close. She'd fallen too hard, and it scared her.

What was she afraid of? Why had she been so hesitant to allow him past the barriers she'd built around herself and her heart?

All her life, her adoptive mother had kept her from playing with others, refusing to let her out of her sight for long. She'd instilled in PJ a lack of trust in people and a determination to live a life independent of others. PJ had found companionship in the horses she loved at the resort stables, volunteering to muck out stalls and exercise the animals.

Chuck had been there, working quietly around her, his love of the animals equal to her own. Over time, he'd overcome her shyness and they'd gone riding together and talked. He'd taught her how to laugh again, something she thought she'd never do. And PJ had fallen in love with the big ex-football jock cowboy, breaking her self-imposed rule not to invest her heart in anyone but to rely solely on herself.

She'd gone so far as to accept his proposal of marriage and actually started dreaming of a wedding and happily ever after.

Until Chuck's National Guard unit had asked for volunteers to deploy and Chuck had raised his hand.

PJ's world had caved in around her. She'd been heartbroken that Chuck would want to leave her and go to war. All she could see in her future was how alone she'd be. Her adoptive mother wouldn't be around forever, her health having deteriorated over the past several years.

She'd been so upset, she'd thrown his ring in his face and told him she never wanted to see him again. Looking back, she realized how childish she'd been.

She hadn't been there to see him off when he'd left for predeployment training. Hadn't told him that she'd missed her period and suspected she was pregnant.

For a short time, PJ thought she could handle being a part of another person's life. But then Chuck had left. Not long afterward, Terri Franks died of a heart attack, leaving her alone in the world, without money or a home to live in. She'd been saving money for years so that someday she could afford to start college online and study animal husbandry. When Terri died, all the money had gone to pay for Terri's funeral.

Terri had been renting the house they lived in. When she'd passed, PJ had gone to work instead of college in order to pay the rent. But the rent had been too much for the meager earnings she'd gotten from the odd jobs she was able to get around town. Without family or a degree and any formal experience, she was destitute and alone. Everyone she'd ever loved was gone, making her promise herself never to get too close to anyone, lest they die and leave her.

Then Charlie came along....

A voice outside her door brought her out of her sad memories and across the room to press her ear to the door. From the deep timbre and pitch, PJ could tell it was Chuck. She peered through the peephole but couldn't see him.

Something shuffled against the outside of the door. What was he doing?

She pressed her ear harder against the door and listened.

"She had a scare, but she's all right," Chuck was saying to someone.

Who was he talking to?

"Whoever broke in tonight won't try again. He'll have to go through me to get to her."

PJ smiled, feeling better about going to sleep now than she had a few moments before.

Apparently Chuck planned to sleep in front of her door.

"We'll talk tomorrow."

Something bumped softly against the door, and all went silent.

PJ pressed a hand to the door. Chuck was on the other side. So close, and yet a huge chasm stretched between them. She'd kept knowledge of his daughter from him.

Even if he forgave her, she wasn't sure she could let him back in her life.

Chapter Three

PJ rose early the next morning, fed Charlie, dressed and loaded the diaper bag with frozen breast milk and diapers for the day care. She had to be at the diner for the first shift.

She dreaded opening the door and waking Chuck after he'd spent the night sleeping in the hall. A twinge of guilt pinched her chest at the thought of him lying on a hard vinyl-tile floor all night, while she'd had a soft mattress and pillows to cushion her.

With the words to thank him poised on her lips, she hooked the infant carrier with Charlie in it on one arm and the diaper bag on the other and eased open the door.

The hallway was empty. Chuck's door was closed. Had he slept outside all night or just part of it?

PJ let go of the breath she'd been holding, relieved she wouldn't have to confront him yet. She'd spent the better part of the rest of her night tossing and turning, thinking about the man who'd attacked her, and more so, the one sleeping on the other side of her door.

She'd known that one day she'd have to tell Chuck about Charlie, and she'd been fully intending to tell him upon his return from his deployment. She thought she had two more months. The day had come sooner than she'd anticipated, and she hadn't been ready.

PJ exited the building and hurried toward her car, hoping she wouldn't run into Chuck outside. Charlie had fallen asleep in her infant carrier even before they'd left the apartment. Her little eyes scrunched as the full force of the morning sunlight shone down on her tiny face.

PJ juggled the carrier to unlock the car. Charlie whimpered but remained asleep.

As she settled the carrier into the car, PJ's skin prickled and the hairs on the back of her neck stood on end. She cast a glance over her shoulder.

No one was there, although she could have sworn a shadow shifted at the corner of the building. Snapping the seat into place, PJ straightened and faced the back of the resort building.

"Anyone there?" she called out, her voice shaky, her knees even shakier.

No answer. A curtain was pushed aside in a window above and Chuck peered down, half of his face covered in shaving cream.

Warmth filled PJ's neck and cheeks. The man was ageless and looked as good today as he had a year ago when she'd been young and stupid in love.

Seeing him standing there with his razor in his hand made PJ's heart turn cartwheels against her ribs.

Chuck disappeared and reappeared at the sliding glass door on the balcony of his room, bare-chested, a towel slung over one shoulder. "Are you okay?" he called out.

The heat built in her cheeks as she nodded. "I'm fine."

"I thought I heard you call out."

"I talk to myself sometimes." Feeling foolish and paranoid, she gave him half a smile. "Gotta go." PJ slipped behind the wheel of her beat-up car and closed the door to avoid further conversation with the father of her child. What else could she say while standing in the parking lot and him hanging over the balcony? *Welcome back? Sorry I didn't tell you about your baby? Or, damn, you look good?*

She shifted into Reverse, backed out of the parking space and pulled out onto the road. A glance in her rearview mirror confirmed that Chuck was still standing on the balcony, watching her. Below, at the corner of the building, something moved. PJ frowned, slowed the vehicle and shot a quick glance over her shoulder at the resort.

Nothing.

She supposed paranoia was bound to be a result of postattack jitters. With a shrug, she turned the corner and drove to the church day care on the other side of town where Charlie spent her days with Dana, who worked there part-time, and the other ladies who ran the child care program. She'd been going there since PJ started to work for Cara Jo at the diner two months prior.

PJ worked mornings, lunch and early afternoon. Late afternoon, she spent either at her computer or in the library taking college courses online.

Dana met her at the door to the infant room. "Running a little late, aren't you?"

PJ dropped the diaper bag on the floor and slid the infant carrier off her arm. Dana took the carrier and set it on a counter, unbuckling Charlie from the restraints. "Hey, sweetie, come see Auntie Dana."

Charlie's eyes blinked open, and she stared up at Dana.

Regret tugged at PJ's heart that she had to spend so much time away from her daughter. But she'd made a commitment to build a better life for herself and Charlie, and the only way she could do that was to get a degree. And she wouldn't have been able to do that if not for the scholarship she'd received from an anonymous benefactor.

Dana lifted Charlie into her arms and stared across her downy hair to PJ. "So, did you meet him?"

"Meet who?" PJ pulled the bottles of breast milk from the diaper bag and settled them into the refrigerator, determined to ignore Dana's questions. Unfortunately, she couldn't stop the slow burn rising in her cheeks at the mere mention of her new neighbor in the resort apartments.

A smile spread across Dana's face. "You did. Isn't he hunky?"

"Dana, you're married. What would Tommy say?"

She shrugged. "I'm married, not dead. And I'm only thinking of you, not myself."

PJ's lips twisted into a half smile. "I know him."

"You do?"

"Yes, we dated for a while."

"Shut up. You're kidding, right? That gorgeous hunk?"

Knowing it would be out before long, PJ kissed Charlie, her heart pinching tight. Then she crossed to the door, her hand resting on the knob, ready to yank and run. "Look, I have to get to work. But you should know that the man you met last night is Charlie's father." She opened the door.

"Oh, no you didn't." Dana advanced on her, carrying Charlie. "You didn't just hit-and-run. You have to stay and tell me everything."

"I can't. I'm already late for work. I promise we'll talk this afternoon when I pick up Charlie."

"Darn right you will." Dana smiled down at Charlie. "And we'll spend all day talking about your daddy, won't we, sweet baby?"

PJ slipped out before she broke down in front of Dana. After the attack last night, the intense joy of seeing Chuck for the first time in almost a year and then breaking the news of Charlie to him, PJ was emotionally wrung out. And she hadn't even pulled her eight-hour shift yet.

She trudged to her car and hurried back the way she'd come, anxious to dive into work so that she could forget everything else.

Ha. As if that would happen. With Chuck hired on as the handyman, she didn't have a chance.

Cara Jo cornered her as soon as she entered the diner with its black and white tiled floor and fifties-style tables and chairs. "I can't believe I slept right through everything."

PJ shook her head. "I take it you heard about the incident last night." She stepped around the counter and tucked her purse behind the stash of paper towels.

"I didn't hear anything. No sirens, no screaming, nothing. I had to hear it from a deputy who'd stopped in for coffee this morning." Cara Jo grabbed PJ's arms. "Are you okay?"

PJ smiled. "I'm here, aren't I?"

"That bastard didn't hurt you?"

A chill rippled across PJ's skin, and she touched the base of her throat where the lamp cord had almost been the death of her. "Not much. Just scared the fool out of me." PJ grabbed a full coffeepot and struck out across the diner, determined to end the conversation. After refilling several empty mugs and taking orders for breakfast, she returned to the counter and Cara Jo, a little more in control of her emotions and ready to launch her own attack. "Why didn't you tell me about Chuck?"

Cara Jo's brows rose innocently. "Chuck?"

"The handyman you hired for the resort?" PJ's brows rose to match Cara Jo's.

"Oh, yeah, him." Cara Jo's cheeks reddened. She rested a hand on PJ's arm. "When Hank told me he'd hired a handyman, I didn't know it was Chuck at first. Hank's my new boss. I didn't have a say. He hired him and told me he'd be starting today. It wasn't until we were on the way to Fort Stockton that Hank let me know who he really was. I swear." She held up her hand, her expression too solemn to be a hoax. Cara Jo had never lied to PJ. Why would she start now?

"Why didn't you warn me then?"

"I was trying to find the words, but for some reason, I never could come up with the right ones." She shrugged. "Are you mad at me?"

PJ sighed. "No. I can't stay mad at you." She set the coffeepot on the burner. "Do you have any say in who works as the handyman?"

"Not yet. I just accepted the position of resort manager. I haven't even had a chance to move my stuff into the office."

PJ sighed. Chuck would be around for a while. "I guess we won't be seeing much of you around the diner once you get oriented with your new duties."

"My first responsibility is to the diner. It's my baby. I won't desert you and the staff here." Cara Jo hugged PJ. "And you'll always be my friend, so don't think you're getting out of this relationship without an argument from me."

Her heart warming at Cara Jo's display of affection, PJ reminded herself how lucky she was to have Cara Jo in her life. When her adoptive mother had died of a heart attack, PJ had felt more alone than she had since she'd come to Wild Oak Canyon. If not for Cara Jo giving her a job and arranging with the resort for a place to live, she and Charlie would have been destitute. Then out of the blue, the scholarship had landed in her lap and PJ felt she was finally on her way to a new and better life for her and her daughter.

The bell over the diner door jingled and PJ glanced up, her heart flipping over.

Chuck entered, his gaze crossing the room to clash with PJ's. Hank Derringer entered behind Chuck and then smiled and nodded toward Cara Jo and PJ. The two settled in the farthest corner in a booth.

"Want me to get them?" Cara Jo asked.

"No. I can do this." PJ stiffened her spine.

"Does Chuck know about Charlie?" Cara Jo whispered.

PJ nodded, gathering two menus and two coffee mugs, her hands shaking. "He found out last night after he chased the attacker out of my apartment."

Cara Jo whistled softly. "Wow, what a way to learn you have a baby daughter."

A stab of guilt twisted in PJ's gut. "Yeah. But what's done is done. I have to live with the choice I made."

"Any chance you two will get back together?" Cara Jo asked.

Her chest tightening so much she could barely breathe, PJ shrugged. She was afraid if she spoke, her voice would crack along with her composure.

"I get it. It's too soon to talk about it." Cara Jo gave her a pat on the back. "Go on. You're tough—you can handle this."

PJ wasn't so sure, but she didn't plan on hiding every time she ran into Chuck. Wild Oak Canyon was too small to think she could avoid him forever.

"ANY OTHER PROBLEMS after last night's initial incident?" Hank asked.

Chuck dragged his gaze away from PJ as she strode across the black and white linoleum tiles of the diner toward them. He had a hard time focusing on Hank with PJ nearby. "What? Oh, no. I checked her balcony door locks and each of the windows and then bedded down in the hallway to make sure no one bothered her again."

Hank sighed. "I figured something might happen, but I wasn't sure what or when."

PJ stopped at their table and set the menus and the empty coffee mugs in front of them. "Coffee?"

"Yes, please." Hank frowned. "Are you all right, my dear?"

PJ smiled down at the older man. "I'm fine, thanks to Chuck. I understand you hired him as the handyman for the resort."

"I did. Thought we could use someone with carpentry skills who could also work with the horses since Juan is no longer with us."

She nodded curtly. "I'll be right back with the coffee."

As soon as PJ was out of earshot, Hank leaned closer. "I don't want anyone to know I hired you to protect PJ. The less connection she has to me, the less chance of her being hurt."

"What's going on? All you told me was that I needed to provide protection to an employee of the resort. What made you think PJ needed protecting?"

"I got a call from an adoption agency in Flagstaff, Arizona. They noted that their computer system had been hacked, and PJ's files had been the target."

"And why would they call you?"

Hank glanced around the diner, his blue eyes darkening. "I knew PJ's birth mother, Alana Rodriguez. She made sure that if anything happened to PJ's adoptive mother, all correspondence or concerns should be directed to me."

"Why you?"

"I helped her escape her abusive fiancé twenty-six years ago in Cozumel, Mexico. It was easy for her to fit into a new life in the United States. She spoke fluent English and had sandy-blond hair and green eyes just like PJ. I suspect her coloring was a throwback from her European Spanish heritage."

Chuck's eyes narrowed. "Something tells me there's more to this story."

Hank sighed. "I told her if she ever needed me for anything to let me know." He stared across the table at Chuck. "When she disappeared, her fiancé had the Mexican police arrest me, claiming I'd murdered Alana."

"What happened to her?"

"I arranged for her to get to the States, gave her a new identity and she disappeared. I didn't see her again."

"How did you get the Mexican government to drop the charges?"

"With no body and no evidence of foul play, they couldn't keep me. Although I barely got out of Mexico."

"So why is this all surfacing again?"

"Her fiancé, Emilio Montalvo," Hank slid a blurry picture of a Hispanic man in front of Hank, "had connections deep in the Mexican Mafia. He swore when he found Alana, he'd make us both pay. I stayed away from her, sure that any contact with her would put her at risk of him finding her. I didn't know she'd had a child and the child was PJ until last year."

"How did you find out?"

Hank's gaze dropped to the empty coffee mug in his hand. "I found out when Terri Franks, a woman I barely knew who'd worked at the resort for the past eight years, died."

"PJ's adoptive mother." Chuck's gaze slipped

from Hank to PJ, headed their way with a carafe of coffee.

Hank turned a smile toward PJ as she stopped to fill his cup.

"Ready to order?" PJ directed her question to Hank, refusing to lock gazes with Chuck.

They had a lot to discuss, but Chuck didn't want to do it in public. It would wait until that evening when he could get her alone.

Hank and Chuck ordered breakfast, and PJ walked away.

"How did you find out PJ was Alana's daughter, not Terri's?"

"I received a package in the mail from Terri Franks's attorney. In it was a letter from Alana, asking me to look out for her daughter should anything happen to Terri. In the letter Terri left with her lawyer, she explained how she'd been PJ's nanny when they lived out in Arizona. Alana had arranged to have Terri adopt PJ if something should happen to her. I only wish I'd known then."

"Why do you think the hacking into the adoption agency's files points to you and PJ?"

"My corporate and personal computer systems were also maliciously hacked. All the data was downloaded to some site in Mexico."

"Was your letter from Alana in those files?"

"No."

"Then how would the hacker connect you to PJ?"

"PJ doesn't know it, but the scholarship she's

going to school on comes from one of my corporations. The bank statements and money trail were part of the system hacked."

"Any leads on who might be hacking into your system, or who might want to hurt PJ?"

"Anyone could be getting to me by targeting PJ."

Chuck drummed his fingers on the table. "But hacking into the adoption files…that makes it a little more personal."

Hank nodded. "Exactly."

"You think Alana's ex-fiancé might have traced PJ through the adoption agency?"

"It's a possibility."

"How long ago did you say it was when you helped this woman, Alana?"

Hank stared across the table at Chuck. "Twenty-six years ago."

Chuck did the math in his head. PJ had turned twenty-five while he'd been in Afghanistan. His gut tightened. "The next question—and I wouldn't ask if I didn't think it might be important—but just who is PJ's father?"

The older man opened his mouth and then closed it and smiled, his head turning toward the woman in question.

"Your breakfast." PJ set a steaming plate of eggs, sunny-side up, in front of Hank and one in front of Chuck, her arm brushing against his, sending sensual shock waves across his senses.

Chuck's fingers tightened on the napkin in his

lap to keep from reaching out and pulling PJ into his arms.

PJ jerked her arm back, her eyes flaring wide for a moment. Her chest rose and fell on a deep breath. "Is there anything else I can get you?" she asked, her voice shaking.

"No, thank you," Hank answered for them both.

Chuck couldn't speak, his throat tight around his vocal cords. He wanted to hold PJ so badly, he had to remain completely still or risk leaping from his seat and taking her into his arms.

When PJ turned and hurried away, Chuck let go of the breath he'd been holding and faced Hank. "Were you and Alana more than just acquaintances?"

Hank nodded.

"So PJ could be your and Alana's daughter."

The older man lifted his fork and put it down again. "I don't know. Without informing PJ of our connection, I don't know how to get a sample for DNA testing. If she's my daughter, she runs the risk of kidnapping attempts."

"Like your wife and son…" Chuck had heard about Hank's family before he'd deployed. Everyone in Wild Oak Canyon knew they'd disappeared two years ago and Hank had been looking for them ever since.

Hank stared across the table at Chuck, his face haggard, older than his fifty-something years. "I couldn't bear for her to be hurt because of me."

"You need to tell her," Chuck said.

"When I know for sure."

"The only way you'll know for sure is to do DNA testing. You'd have to tell her something to get the sample you need."

Hank threw his napkin on the table, his brows furrowed. "I couldn't bear it if someone targeted another person because of me."

"She might not be yours at all. Alana could have had another relationship with someone else shortly after disappearing."

Hank's eyes narrowed. "Then why leave the letter for me?"

"She counted on you to help." Chuck stared across the room at PJ, leaning close to an elderly woman, taking her order. "What if PJ is the ex-fiancé's daughter?"

"Things might get even worse." Hank's lips tightened. "He'll want what is his and will stop at nothing to take her and the child."

Chapter Four

PJ felt as if she was walking on eggshells the entire time Chuck and Hank were eating their breakfast. Several times she fumbled coffee mugs, almost dropping them.

"Hey, it's okay." Cara Jo rested a hand on her arm. "The world will not come to an end because the old fiancé is back in town."

"I know. But we haven't had *the talk* yet. I don't know what he's going to want in the way of visitation with Charlie." PJ wrung her hands, staring at Chuck's back. "He might sue for custody, for all I know."

Cara Jo clucked her tongue. "Don't borrow trouble, sweetie. He doesn't strike me as the vindictive type."

"No, but he's always wanted children. He'll want to be a part of Charlie's life."

"And that's a problem?" Cara Jo's brows rose. "Honey, a girl needs a daddy in her life. Not that you wouldn't do a good job of raising her. But having a good male role model sets her up for future relationships and expectations of the kind of men she should date."

"Charlie's only three months old, for God's sake." PJ flung her hands in the air. "I'm not ready for my baby to start dating."

Cara Jo chuckled. "I know. But having a good role model early in her life gives her a firm foundation when it comes to the kind of guy she might one day marry."

PJ pinched the bridge of her nose, a headache forming at the thought of Charlie as a teen. "I don't want to think about Charlie dating or marrying until at least after the terrible twos."

"Order up!" Mrs. Kinsley yelled through the window from the kitchen.

Cara Jo handed her two plates of biscuits and gravy. "Sadly, it'll be here before you know it. Take these to table nine, while I see if I can help Mrs. Kinsley catch up."

PJ threw herself into taking orders and delivering food, busing tables in between. The hectic pace kept her too busy for her eyes to stray to the corner where Chuck and Hank sat, taking their sweet time over coffee. Still, her gaze found its way there every time she turned around.

Chuck's broad shoulders and the high-and-tight military haircut made butterflies swarm in her belly and stirred the longing she'd thought was buried with the letters from Chuck she'd kept in a box beneath her bed.

She hadn't opened them for fear she'd lose her determination and conviction that she was doing the right thing by moving on. Yet she hadn't returned them or thrown them away. At first, he'd sent a letter every other day after he'd deployed to Afghanistan. When she refused to respond, the letters slowed to a trickle until about a month before Charlie was born, when they'd stopped altogether.

In her eighth month of pregnancy, PJ had never felt more alone. Sure, Cara Jo had been beside her, had gone to prenatal classes with her and coached her through the actual delivery, but it wasn't the same.

The guilt of not having told Chuck of the baby and her continued longing gnawed at her heart. She hadn't wanted to give her heart to him, knowing he'd leave her and possibly never come back. With her luck, he'd die just like every other presumably permanent person in her life. Her mother, what little she remembered of her, and her adoptive mother. Hell, she had never known her father.

Now she had Charlie in her life, and every day she worried that something horrible would happen to her. And it almost had the night before.

On her break PJ retreated to the diner office to use the telephone and dialed the number for the day care.

"Heavenly Hope Day Care, this is Dana."

"Oh, good," PJ breathed. "Just the person I wanted to talk to."

"PJ?"

"I know it's overprotective of me, but I had to call and check on Charlie."

"I'm holding her in my arms as we speak. She's just fine." Dana paused. "How about you? You sound a bit shaken."

"I guess I am after last night's attack."

The phone clattered and Dana muttered an expletive before saying, "Sorry, dropped the phone. Now, what do you mean *attack?* You didn't say anything about it when you dropped Charlie off. Did Chuck attack you?"

PJ shoved a hand through her hair and sighed. "Sorry, Dana. I must have forgotten, what with Chuck being there and all."

"Did he hurt you?"

"No. Chuck came in and saved the day." PJ glanced around the office. "I have to get back to work. I just wanted to know Charlie was okay."

"I'll keep an extra special eye on her and let you know of anything out of the ordinary. Sheesh. Attacked? You better fill me in on *all* the details this afternoon."

"I will."

"That's something a girl doesn't forget. I guess having Chuck around has you completely rattled."

"You don't know the half of it." PJ said her goodbyes and hung up. When she returned to the dining room, her gaze went straight to the empty corner booth.

The tension eased from her shoulders, and she let go of the breath she'd been holding for what felt like the entire morning.

The sooner she got used to having Chuck around, the better. No doubt, knowing he had a child, the big cowboy wasn't going anywhere for a while.

The rest of the morning passed quickly with customers straggling in for late breakfast and then into the lunch hours. PJ glanced toward the door every time the bell above it jingled, half expecting Chuck to stride through.

Her nerves were shot by the time the lunch crowd thinned and she hung up her apron. "If you don't mind, I have to leave early to get some errands done and study before I pick up Charlie at the day care."

Cara Jo smiled. "No problem. I can handle the cleanup. Go on. And PJ..."

PJ slipped her purse strap over her shoulder and faced Cara Jo.

"Things will turn out for the best. Just you wait and see." Cara Jo hugged her.

PJ returned the hug, her vision blurred with ready tears. "I hope so." She left the diner and climbed the back stairs to her apartment over the resort. The shadowy hallway made her hurry along, her key at the ready.

When she stepped into the apartment, her gaze darted all around the postage stamp-size living-room-and-kitchen combo. The normal scents of talcum powder and baby shampoo held a hint of aftershave.

PJ shivered and wondered when that smell would dissipate. She vowed to throw open the windows when she got home that evening to air it out.

As she grabbed her notebook and papers from her corner desk, she paused. The photo album she kept on the shelf above her ancient computer stuck out a little more than usual. It hadn't been that way that morning when she'd straightened her desk before heading for work.

Her chest tightened as a chill slipped across the back of her neck, making the tiny hairs stand on end. How long would it take to erase the memory of a man breaking and entering her home? Not only had her apartment been breached, but her safe haven had also been compromised.

Every little thing that seemed out of place would get more scrutiny. PJ shoved aside her paranoia and left, carefully locking the door. As a second thought, she tore off a corner of one of her papers and slipped it between the door and jamb above the lock. If someone broke in, the paper would be displaced. Call her crazy, but she needed some measure of security, and though minuscule, the little trick left her feeling a little more in control.

Her apartment behind her, PJ climbed into her car and headed for the law offices of Hanes and Taylor. She had to know what her rights were and what she might face if Chuck decided he wanted custody of Charlie.

Even the slimmest chance of losing custody of her baby had PJ's gut so knotted she could hardly breathe.

THROUGHOUT THE DAY, Chuck worked on projects ranging from replacing rotted eaves to mucking stalls. In between tasks, he made it a habit to swing by the diner's wide windows to peek in at PJ.

So many times during his tour in Afghanistan he'd dreamed of seeing PJ again, of holding her in his arms. In his imagination, he could hear her voice telling him she'd been wrong, that she wanted him in her life no matter what profession he chose.

Those dreams had helped him hold it together during the dangerous missions. The thought of coming back to Wild Oak Canyon to salvage his relationship with the woman he loved ended in a hero's welcome. Such were his dreams.

The reality was, PJ had lied to him by withholding information about Charlie. If Chuck hadn't returned to Wild Oak Canyon, he'd never have known he had a daughter.

His chest swelled as he thought of the tiny baby, lying in her crib, her soft tuft of hair like silk against his fingers.

He'd smashed his fingers with a hammer more than once, losing his focus over little Charlie. And the more he saw PJ through the window, the more he alternated between wanting to hold her and wanting to shake her.

Around noon, he ducked into the resort office.

The young woman manning the counter, barely out of her teens, smiled. "May I help you?"

Chuck read the name tag. "Hi, Alicia. I'm Chuck, the new handyman."

Alicia reached across the counter and shook Chuck's hand. "Welcome to Wild Oak Canyon Resort."

"Do you know of any repairs that need to be made in any of the rooms?"

The young woman behind the counter smiled and shrugged. "I only work part-time in the afternoons after my classes get out at the community college, so I don't always get the 4-1-1. You'll have to ask the new manager."

"Ms. Smithson?" Chuck asked.

"Yes, sir. You can find her at the diner until about two. Then she'll be back in her office at the resort."

Chuck glanced at the old-fashioned guest register on the counter, committing the names on the list to memory. Perhaps one of the guests was PJ's attacker. "Are there many guests this time of year?"

"It's a slow season, from what they tell me. Only about twenty-five people are here for the week. Many are planning to attend the rodeo in the neighboring town. We get the overflow."

Chuck made a note to work with Cara Jo to review

the list of guests and to get Hank to run a background check on any who might be questionable. Since the attack had just happened only the night before, whoever did it could be new in town, thus needing a place to stay. One close enough where he could study PJ's every move. Chuck's fists tightened. The sooner he discovered the culprit and put him in jail—or out of his misery—the better. "I guess I'll be seeing you around, Alicia."

"Nice to meet you."

Chuck went back to work in the stable. By early afternoon, he'd finished mucking stalls and was just emptying a wheelbarrow full of manure in the pile behind the stables when he saw PJ's car pull out of the rear parking lot of the resort. Even if he hadn't been tasked with protecting the confounded woman, curiosity got the better of him.

Chuck dusted off his jeans, climbed into his truck and followed. Wild Oak Canyon wasn't a big enough town to boast a single stoplight. A couple of dozen streets crisscrossed in straight lines on the flat terrain.

PJ pulled into a building a few blocks from the diner.

Chuck waited at a stop sign until PJ went inside before he passed. His heart skipped several beats when he read the sign in front of the neat little house, converted into a business. Hanes and Taylor, Attorneys at Law.

Was that the way she'd play this? Anger spiked

as he turned the corner and circled the block. Most likely she was getting legal advice about child custody.

As Chuck rounded the block and came back out on Main, PJ's car was pulling away from the curb. She hadn't had time to consult with anyone. She had probably only set up an appointment.

Chuck's jaw tightened. Tonight, he and PJ would have a talk about Charlie's future. A future that would include Chuck, by God.

Feeling a bit guilty over stalking PJ, Chuck left a big gap between his truck and her car.

PJ's next stop was on the other side of town at a quaint little church with a fenced playground out back and a sign out front with the words painted in block letters, Heavenly Hope Day Care.

Chuck kept his distance, parking in an abandoned gas station until PJ came out.

Twenty minutes later, he'd about given up when PJ emerged carrying an infant car seat, Charlie's little head barely visible over the sides. Her tiny hand waved at the sky, bringing a smile to Chuck's face.

He wanted to hold his little girl, to get to know her and watch her grow.

Had PJ not shut him out of her life, Chuck would have moved heaven and earth to be there when Charlie came into the world. He sighed. Then again, the army didn't always let soldiers out of their deployments for the births of their children. Even had PJ told him he was going to be a father, he probably wouldn't have gotten a furlough to return home for the event.

He could understand some of the reasoning behind PJ keeping the birth of his child from him. But Charlie was three months old. Chuck had been back in the States for a month of that, in the hospital for rehab and then processing out of the military.

After almost a year's separation, he'd thought he'd be over PJ, but that was as far from the truth as he could get.

The woman had never been far from his mind, and his job of protecting her would only put them closer still.

Chuck considered asking Hank to pull him from this case. But who did he know he could trust to guarantee PJ's safety? And who had as much at stake when it came to Charlie?

If the Mexican Mafia was after PJ and Charlie, he'd need a friggin' army to surround her, especially in this part of south Texas where drugs traveled across the border seemingly unconstrained. There were enough Mafia members on both sides of the border that if they wanted PJ and Charlie, one cowboy wasn't going to stop them. Chuck wondered if the four cowboys Hank had hired made up the entirety of Covert Cowboys, Inc., or if Hank had additional help he hadn't met yet.

Chuck stayed behind PJ as she drove back to her apartment. He gave her five minutes to unload and get into her room before he parked and climbed out.

The more he thought about PJ and Charlie being at risk with the Mexican Mafia, the more he needed to know about those he might be up against. A visit with Hank's computer guru who had access to just about anything that had a computer footprint was in order. But first, he had to make sure PJ and Charlie would be okay.

Chuck scanned the parking lot, noting all the shadowy areas a person could hide to ambush an unsuspecting mother. He made notes to himself to trim back bushes and install motion-sensor lighting to ward off surprise attacks. Since he, PJ and Cara Jo were the only people who should be parking behind the buildings, safety in numbers wasn't really an option.

At the top of the staircase leading to the pair of apartments he and PJ occupied, Chuck paused and surveyed the hallway. The light overhead gave a dingy glow. He'd clean the globe and change the bulbs.

He paused with his fist hovering over PJ's door and got a good whiff of his own stench. After mucking horse manure for part of the day, he probably smelled like the stuff.

Chuck turned back toward his apartment when PJ's door jerked open.

"I knew it."

Chuck spun to face her.

She had Charlie in her arms and a scowl on her face. "You were following me, weren't you?"

Chuck couldn't lie to her. "Yes."

"I don't need a keeper, so back off."

"Are you mad because I followed you or because I saw that you stopped at an attorney's office?" he threw back at her.

Charlie batted at her mother's face, blowing bubbles with her spit.

Chuck had a hard time staying mad when the baby drew his attention out of the fight.

"I only made an appointment. I figured we'd have to have some kind of agreement written up over visitation with Charlie."

"We still need to have that talk."

PJ sighed. "I know."

"But let me get a shower first. I smell like hell."

PJ's nose twitched, the hint of a smile tugging at her lips. "You really do."

Chuck's heart flipped. He'd missed her smile. "Five minutes."

"Just knock."

Chuck hurriedly collected his toiletries and ducked beneath the hot spray, scrubbing away a day of hard work. It had been a long time since he'd worked with horses and barnyards. His muscles were stiff from shoveling. Other than digging foxholes, he hadn't had to shovel much in the army, and he could tell the muscles had been neglected. And his bum leg ached like hell.

He let the warm water pepper his muscles as he

collected his thoughts for the coming confrontation with PJ.

Showered and dressed in clean clothes, he knocked on PJ's door.

"Just a minute," she called out.

A moment later, she opened the door, again holding Charlie. "Sorry. We were in the middle of Charlie's supper." PJ tugged her T-shirt down over her hip.

It took a moment for Chuck to digest her meaning. When it hit him that she had been breastfeeding Charlie, his face heated.

PJ folded a cloth over his shoulder and held Charlie out. "Here, you can burp her while I fix something to eat." Once he'd taken the baby, she performed an about-face and hurried toward the kitchenette in the corner. "I hope you like spaghetti. It's cheap and easy to fix."

"I didn't expect you to cook for me."

She shrugged. "It's just as easy to cook spaghetti for two as for one person."

Chuck still held Charlie out at arm's length. "How do I burp her?"

PJ chuckled. "Lay her over your shoulder and pat her back. She'll do the rest."

No sooner had Chuck laid her over his shoulder than Charlie burped.

"See?" PJ turned with a wooden spoon in her hand. "Easy."

"All I did was put her on my shoulder."

"Sometimes that's all it takes." She waved the spoon. "Pat her back anyway. She probably has another one in there."

In awe and a little afraid of the tiny bundle of baby, Chuck patted her back gently, afraid he'd break her little body with his big hand.

"Oh, come on, she won't break. Give her a firm pat."

Chuck patted her back again, this time a little harder. Nothing happened.

"Don't stop. She likes it."

As he patted her back, Chuck paced across the small room and back, sure he was doing it wrong. Finally Charlie burped again and cooed.

The sound made Chuck's heart skip several beats. "Is that normal?"

"That's her way of saying thank you. I told you, she likes it."

Chuck glanced at PJ standing with her back to him. She seemed to be thinner than he remembered. "How was it?"

"What?"

"Your pregnancy, the delivery? I want to know."

"I did fine. I guess my body is built for bearing children. No health issues and a natural delivery."

He wanted to know more, but he clamped down on his tongue to keep from asking too many personal questions. "I would have been there…"

"I know you would have. If you could have."

"Why didn't you tell me?" He tipped Charlie into

the crook of his arm and stared down into her little face.

"You weren't here. You wouldn't have been here even had you known." Her hand stopped stirring the sauce, and she stood for a long moment, unmoving. "Your focus needed to be on staying alive. What was the point in telling you?"

His anger stirred again. "The point is, I'm Charlie's father."

"And if there had been complications, what could you have done from Afghanistan?"

Chuck sighed. "Nothing."

A long silence stretched between them.

"I won't try to keep you from seeing Charlie," PJ said.

Chuck stared up at PJ. She'd lied by omission about Charlie. Would she lie about trying to keep him from seeing his daughter? What about the visit to the attorney? Was she only trying to set an agreement in place, or was she preparing to cut him out of Charlie's life?

At this point, Hank didn't want her to know Chuck had been hired as her bodyguard, not as a handyman as he'd told PJ.

PJ glanced at him and sighed. Then she held her hand up, spoon and all. "I swear on my mothers' graves I won't keep you from Charlie. There. Are you satisfied?"

Chuck nodded. He liked the strong, determined woman she'd grown into in the year he'd been away, and found himself even more attracted to her than before. "Okay. I trust you." He might trust her about visitation with Charlie, but he wasn't as sure about where they stood, or if he trusted her with his heart. Was attraction enough?

"Trust or not, it's the truth." She turned back to the stove. "You about ready for dinner?"

Chuck gazed down at the baby sleeping in his arms. He didn't want to let go of her even to eat supper. "I guess."

PJ chuckled. "Does my cooking reputation precede me? I'm not Cara Jo, but I can—"

Footsteps pounded on the staircase and then in the hallway outside PJ's apartment door.

PJ turned to Chuck. "Give me Charlie." She held out her hands for the baby.

Chuck handed her over and motioned for her to get behind him. "Go into the bedroom and close the door."

PJ did as she was told, her eyes wide, her face pale. As she closed the bedroom door, someone pounded on the door to the apartment.

"Help! Please, help!" a female voice called out, followed by loud sobs.

Chuck peered through the peephole and then yanked the door open.

The young woman from the resort front desk fell against his chest, her face streaked with tears. "Please help him."

Chapter Five

Chuck caught the woman and held her as she sobbed into his chest. "Help who?"

"Danny, my boyfriend. He's hurt." She sniffed and pushed her hair out of her face. "He's at the bottom of the stairs. I don't know if he's breathing."

Chuck shoved the woman into the apartment. "Stay here and call 9-1-1, and lock the door behind me."

The woman nodded, her hands shaking.

PJ, still carrying Charlie, flung her bedroom door open. "What's wrong? What's happening?"

"I don't know. I'll be right back." Without waiting for her response, Chuck slipped past the distraught woman and lumbered down the stairs two at a time, jolting his bad leg with each step. He almost fell over the crumpled body at the bottom.

The light over the stairs wasn't working, but the glow from the security light in the rear parking lot shone enough on the inert form that Chuck could see a pool of blood.

As he felt for a pulse, Chuck glanced around to

ensure whoever had done this wasn't waiting to do it again.

After several long seconds, he could detect the weak beat of the young man's heart. Rather than hurt him further, he carefully checked for injuries without moving him. The blood appeared to be coming from a wound to the forehead, which would explain why he was unconscious.

Within minutes, sirens wailed from the direction of Wild Oak Canyon's small hospital. A sheriff's vehicle whipped into the parking lot before the ambulance, lights blazing.

A man in uniform leaped out, gun drawn. "Step away from the body," he called out.

"I'm the one who had you called." Chuck didn't recognize the man from the previous night's call.

"Still, step away from the body until we secure the area."

Chuck held up his hands and stepped out into the parking lot. "He's alive, seems to be breathing on his own, but he appears to have suffered a blow to the head."

The ambulance bumped over the rough pavement and came to a halt. Two emergency medical technicians jumped out. One opened a side panel and extracted a medical kit while the other unloaded a backboard.

Cara Jo rounded the corner of the building, her eyes wide. When she spotted Chuck, she hurried to his side. "What the hell's going on?"

"I'm not sure. You know almost as much as I do. The young man's name is Danny. His girlfriend, Alicia, the young woman who works part-time at the front desk of the resort, found him and let us know he'd been hurt."

"I know Danny. He's a nice kid. Who'd want to hurt him?" Cara Jo shook her head.

"Good question."

"Holy hell." Cara Jo shoved her hand through her hair. "Two attacks in as many days. I don't get it."

"Me, either. But tomorrow, this handyman is putting in some additional security measures."

"Glad to hear it. I'm sure the boss won't mind footing that bill. Especially when his employees are being mauled." Cara Jo laid a hand on Chuck's arm. "PJ and Charlie are okay, aren't they?"

"Yes. I was with them when Alicia showed up at the door. Alicia and PJ are upstairs now, if you want to check on them. The deputy will want to speak with the one who found Danny. Maybe you could bring Alicia down as soon as the EMTs get him loaded into the ambulance."

"I'll do that." Cara Jo waited while the EMTs checked vitals and carefully maneuvered the injured man onto the backboard, stabilized his neck and lifted him onto a gurney.

Once the stairway was cleared, the diner owner sprinted up the stairs.

Chuck and the deputy followed the injured man

as he was rolled across the rough pavement. Danny's eyes blinked open as they neared the ambulance.

"Wait." The deputy touched the arm of one of the medical technicians. The gurney came to a smooth halt, and the officer leaned over the gurney. "Son, can you describe the man who attacked you?"

The young man blinked again, and then his eyes rolled upward and he slipped into unconsciousness.

The emergency personnel loaded Danny into the back of the ambulance and climbed in beside him.

Cara Jo was leading a distraught Alicia down the steps.

When Alicia reached the bottom, she ran toward the ambulance. "Is he going to be okay? Can I ride with him?"

"Are you a member of his family, ma'am?" the attendant asked.

She shook her head, wringing her hands. "No, but he's my boyfriend."

"I'm sorry, only family members." The technician closed the door.

Cara Jo slipped an arm around Alicia's shoulders. "Don't worry. I'll give you a ride to the hospital."

The deputy shook his head. "I'll need to ask her a few questions first."

The ambulance pulled away, and tears fell anew from Alicia's eyes.

"I'm Deputy Farnam. I'm sorry about your boyfriend," the policeman offered. "He's in good hands. Can you tell me what happened here?"

"Danny and I were supposed to meet back here after I got off work this evening. Only I was a little late because I had to check in a new guest as I was about to close the office.

"I was in a hurry, afraid Danny would think I'd stood him up. When I came around the side of the building, at first I didn't see anyone. Then I heard Danny shout. He was standing in the shadows by the stairs. Someone dressed in dark clothes and a ski mask was halfway up the stairs. He came down and hit Danny with what looked like a stick." Alicia shook her head, tears making rivulets across her smooth cheeks. "I screamed. The man turned on me. I couldn't move." She shook her head, her eyes wide. "My feet wouldn't budge. The man practically ran over me."

"Did he hurt you?" the officer asked.

"No." Alicia stared at the officer, her face pale, her eyes glassy. "His shoulder bumped me and spun me around. By the time I regained my balance, the man was gone. And Danny…that's when I ran up the stairs to get help." Alicia's voice caught on a sob. "Danny's going to be okay, isn't he?"

"Officer, do you need anything else from Alicia?" Cara Jo hugged the young woman. "I'd like to take her to the hospital."

"Will you be available to sign a statement tomorrow?" he asked.

"Sure." Alicia wiped the tears from her face, her

lips thinning. "Anything to catch the bastard who did this to Danny."

Cara Jo led Alicia around the side of the building.

"Chuck?" PJ touched his arm.

He spun to face her. She held Charlie in her arms. The baby's eyes blinked at the bright lights spinning on the police car.

Chuck wanted to pull PJ and Charlie into his arms and hold them. After listening to Alicia's account, Chuck had no doubt that the attacker was headed up the stairs to get to PJ's apartment, his intentions obviously nefarious.

"Are you okay?" PJ asked, her brows furrowed, her arms tightening around Charlie.

"I'm fine. Although I'm not sure how Alicia's boyfriend will be."

A shout went up from another officer who'd arrived after the first. He held something up in the air.

Deputy Farnam shook his head. "I think we found the weapon our perp used."

The other deputy closed the distance between them, carrying a tire iron. It caught the light where wet blood still clung to the metal.

PJ gasped. "He hit Danny with a tire iron?"

"That's what it looks like." The other deputy held the tire iron with gloved hands. "I hope we can lift prints. I found it in the dust."

PJ stroked Charlie's downy head and pressed a kiss to her chubby cheek.

"You'd better get her inside. I can't believe we didn't hear the attack while it was happening."

"We had the fan over the stove going. You can't hear anything outside over that."

"True. Go on. I'll be up in a minute," Chuck promised. He wanted to talk to the sheriff's deputy before he left.

PJ climbed the stairs, her gaze sweeping the parking lot as she disappeared into the building.

After explaining to the deputies that this had been the second attack in as many days, he asked if they would provide more surveillance in the area until they found the culprit.

"I don't think Danny was the intended victim," he told Farnam.

"I can have a unit come by once every hour until daylight."

Chuck thanked him and then returned to PJ's apartment.

He wouldn't take any more chances. He'd be staying with them tonight.

PJ LAID CHARLIE in her crib and tucked a blanket around her, and then she paced.

When Alicia had told her the same story she'd told the sheriff's deputy, a solid, heavy weight settled in the pit of PJ's gut. The attacker had been headed up the steps. The only people living at the top were Chuck, PJ and Charlie.

She rubbed the gooseflesh rising on her arms.

Since her apartment had been the one broken into the night before, it stood to reason her apartment was once again the target.

Why? Who would want to hurt her or Charlie? She didn't owe anyone money. She hadn't made anyone mad at the diner—at least not mad enough to take a tire iron to her. Had Danny not stopped him…

Chuck had been there. But who was to say the attacker wouldn't have surprised him, armed with a pretty convincing weapon?

PJ stopped in the middle of the floor, hugging her arms around herself, wishing Chuck would finish his business with the cops and come back up the stairs. Not that she expected him to stay in her apartment, but having him nearby gave her more of a sense of safety than if she lived alone in this isolated part of the resort.

Footsteps sounded in the hallway outside, and a light knock sent PJ scooting across the floor. Her hand braced on the doorknob, she hesitated and then looked through the peephole.

Chuck's handsome face filled PJ's view, and she ripped open the door and threw herself into his arms. "Thank God."

He held her, stroking her hair for a moment, and then edged her through the door and closed it behind them.

"What's happening?" she whispered, her fingers clutching at his shirt, refusing to let go.

"I don't know," Chuck said, his voice rumbling against PJ's ear. "But whatever it is, I don't like it."

A tiny whimper sounded from the bedroom.

Chuck gripped PJ's shoulders. "I'll get her."

PJ unwound her fingers from his shirt, pulled herself upright and stepped out of the warmth and safety of Chuck's arms.

The big cowboy filled the doorway to PJ's bedroom as he entered to collect the baby, who had started crying softly.

"Hey, didn't anyone ever tell you that cowgirls don't cry?" He lifted her as if she were a fragile doll, afraid his big old hands would somehow break her. Just as carefully, he tucked her into the crook of his arm, her body so tiny next to his hulk.

She turned her face into his shirt, making sucking motions and then jamming her fist into her mouth.

Chuck grinned. "I think she's hungry."

PJ hurried toward them. "I'll feed her. You don't have to stay."

"I'll just wait in the other room." His face heated. He wasn't a prude, and he'd seen PJ's breasts before. Hell, he'd touched them and nibbled on the tips, making love to her. But they weren't together anymore, and watching her breastfeed Charlie, well, just wouldn't be right. He handed Charlie to her mother and left the bedroom.

PJ closed the door, leaving a little bit of a gap, and settled on the bed.

Chuck wandered around the little living room, checking the doors and windows, even though he'd done the same the night before. He couldn't rest until he knew PJ and Charlie were safe.

He pulled back the curtains over the sliding glass door and tested the latch by pulling on the handle. The door shimmied and held, but with a little muscle behind it, it would give. He made a note to install a new latch. In the meantime, he found a broom in the miniature pantry and broke off the bristled end.

"Did you just break my broom?"

"Yes." He glanced toward the bedroom.

The light in the room cast a soft glow over PJ as Charlie lay clutched to her breast. PJ pressed her fingers against her skin and pulled Charlie off, and then she moved her around to the other side and lifted her shirt.

The baby latched on.

Chuck sucked in a breath, the miracle of a woman's body—of PJ's body—rocking him to the core.

"That's the only broom I had." She glanced up, her gaze capturing Chuck's.

He spun away, blood burning in his cheeks. "I'll buy you another." He jammed the pole between the door frame and the sliding door. Again he tested the sliding door. This time it didn't budge at all. If someone wanted to come in, he'd have to break the glass.

Movement behind him made him turn.

PJ stood with Charlie cradled in her arms. "Could you watch her while I shower?"

Chuck took the baby, his knuckles brushing against PJ's, sending bursts of awareness through his system like tiny electric shocks. "Leave the apartment door open."

PJ GATHERED A TOWEL, toiletries, clean pajamas and the baby monitor, out of habit, and stepped out into the hallway. She turned, her brow furrowing, and stared back into her apartment, which was quickly being taken over by Chuck and his overwhelmingly large presence.

The cowboy settled into her favorite rocking chair, laying Charlie over his shoulder. He glanced at her. "What are you waiting for? Charlie and I will be fine."

"Are you sure I should leave the door open? Won't that put Charlie at risk?"

"I'll take care of Charlie, but I can't take care of you if I don't know whether or not you're in trouble."

"I don't need you to take care of me," she said, a mutinous frown settling on her face. Then it slid away. "But thanks."

She hurried from the apartment, but she couldn't walk away from how she was starting to feel about the big galoot. Starting…no, she'd never stopped having feelings for Chuck. All through the long year of separation, her pregnancy and the first few months of Charlie's life, she'd thought about Chuck and how it could have been. So many times she'd pulled the box of letters he'd written out from under her bed, only to push them back. What was done was done. Her total focus had to be on Charlie.

As she stepped beneath the shower's spray, a little voice in the back of her head kept telling her that Chuck was back, and he wasn't in the military.

Or was he still in the Guard, subject to call-up? She wouldn't know if she didn't ask. If he was still part of the military, nothing had changed. He could be deployed again, this time leaving her *and* Charlie.

The more Charlie grew and got to know her daddy, the more difficult it would be when Chuck left. And PJ would be the one to pick up the pieces and explain to her daughter why her father couldn't be with her.

The image of Chuck sitting in the rocking chair, holding Charlie as if he had been born to be a father, had left an indelible mark on PJ's memories.

PJ didn't have the right to keep Charlie from her father.

The stress of the past twenty-four hours had taken its toll, giving her a stiff neck and a headache. She stood for a long time under the hot spray of the showerhead, until the muscles loosened and the pounding against her temple reduced to a throb.

When the water turned cold, she flipped the

shower off and toweled dry. As she stepped out of the tub, a crackling sound made her jump.

The light glowed red on the monitor. She'd forgotten to turn it off. Now she smiled, imagining she'd heard the creak of the rocking chair.

Then static blasted her again, followed by heavy breathing.

PJ froze, clutching the towel to her chest.

Then in a low, whispered monotone, a voice said, "Who's your daddy, little girl?"

PJ screamed and ran for the door. Whoever had spoken was in the apartment with the base unit and Charlie, and it didn't sound like Chuck.

Without thinking, she flung open the shared bathroom door and ran into a solid wall of muscles.

Terror seized her, and she fought to get past the barrier.

"Charlie."

"Is asleep in her crib." Chuck lifted the edges of the towel she still clutched and wrapped them around her naked body. "Calm down and tell me what happened."

"Was it you?" PJ gripped his shirt. "Tell me it was you."

Chuck shook his head. "I'm sorry, PJ. I don't know what you're talking about."

"The monitor. Did you speak into the baby monitor? Did you say 'Who's your daddy, little girl?'"

He captured her hands in his. "What monitor? What are you talking about?"

"Oh, dear God, let me by. Charlie's in there with him."

Chuck's brows dipped. "What do you mean? I just laid her down in her crib, checked all the windows, closets and under the bed. She's okay."

Tears dribbled from the corners of PJ's eyes. "Please. I have to know for sure."

"Come on." Chuck turned and led the way into the tiny bedroom crowded with a double bed and a baby crib.

PJ leaned over the crib, bumping into the musical mobile, making it play several notes before it stopped.

Charlie's eyes blinked open and she whimpered.

Her heart still hammering, PJ reached into the crib and gathered her daughter into her arms. "Oh, baby. It's okay. Mommy won't let that ol' bad man get you."

Chuck stood in the doorway, his eyes narrowed. "You mind telling me what all that was about?"

Holding Charlie close, still wearing nothing but a towel, PJ stared over her head at Chuck. "Someone spoke into the baby monitor." She closed her eyes for a moment and let go of the breath trapped in her lungs since hearing that terrifying voice. She opened them and stared at the dresser beside the crib. Blood rushed from PJ's head, and she swayed.

"PJ?" Chuck slipped an arm around her waist to steady her. "Are you okay?"

She pointed to the dresser. "The base unit is gone."

"The intruder could have taken it last night."

Before he finished talking, PJ was shaking her head. "No, it was there this morning."

Chapter Six

Chuck checked behind the dresser and under the crib. "Are you sure?"

"Yes. I'd knocked it off the dresser with the diaper bag when I was getting ready this morning. I set it upright before I left." She pointed to the dresser. "It was there. I know it."

"Baby monitors probably don't have much of a range." Chuck's muscles bunched. "Wait here." He spun and raced for the door.

"Where are you going?" she called after him.

"To find the base unit and the guy playing with it."

"Are you crazy?"

Chuck didn't respond. He ducked into his apartment, grabbed a flashlight and his Glock from on top of his dresser, removed the trigger guard and then raced down the stairs, jumping the last four to the bottom. In the parking lot, he spun in a 360-degree circle, searching for movement. When nothing, not even a stray cat, budged in the darkness, Chuck headed for the scrub brush on the edges of the pavement. Whoever was tormenting PJ had probably taken off. After a few minutes, Chuck had checked behind every cactus and yucca plant and found nothing. Then his flashlight beam glanced off something white, half-hidden beneath a squat saw palmetto. He kicked it with his boot.

Lying at his feet was the battery-powered base unit for the baby monitor.

Chuck removed his T-shirt, wrapped it around the monitor and carried it back up the steps, stashing it in his apartment. He'd have Hank run a check for fingerprints. If the guy was the same one who'd hurt Danny, he had a lot of nerve coming back so soon. Unless he'd been among the onlookers gathered around the ambulance and police cars. He double-checked the Glock Hank had assigned him from Co-vert Cowboy, Inc.'s arsenal of weapons. He ejected the clip, checked that it was fully loaded and then slid it back into the handle and checked the safety. He stuffed it into the back of his jeans, pulled his T-shirt over it and left his apartment.

He knocked on PJ's door.

She yanked it open, her eyes wide, her gaze going past him to the empty hallway beyond. Her body wilted, and her brow furrowed. "I take it you didn't find him?"

"No, but I found the base unit. I'll have it checked for fingerprints tomorrow. It's in my apartment for now."

"Well, I'm glad you didn't find him." She held

the door open and stepped to the side. "He could have hurt you like he hurt Danny."

Chuck's lips quirked upward in the corners. "I'm a little bigger than Danny. I think I can handle this guy."

"As long as he's not carrying a gun. Who's to say he won't attack again?"

Chuck shook his head. "After two incidents in one night, I doubt he'll be back again tonight." He pulled the gun from his waistband and laid it on the counter in the kitchen. "And if he comes with a gun, I'll be ready."

Her eyes rounding like saucers, PJ held up her hands. "You can't leave that there. What if it goes off? It could hit Charlie."

"I know how to use the gun, and it's safe as long as you treat it with respect." Chuck lifted the weapon and turned it over. "This is the safety switch to keep you from firing it accidentally. When you have to shoot, you flip it like this, point the gun at your target and pull the trigger. It's simple. Get familiar with it, in case you have to use it. And always be prepared to kill whatever you're aiming at."

"I know how to shoot a gun." PJ's face paled and her hands shook as Chuck laid the Glock in her palms. She knew how to use it, but she wasn't sure she could. PJ had the gun she'd found in her adoptive mother's nightstand. It remained in a box on a shelf, high in PJ's closet, away from Charlie.

"Just hold it for now. I'll take you out to Hank's for target practice soon."

"I told you, I know how to shoot. I just don't like to." PJ weighed the weapon in her palms and shook her head again. "Take it."

Chuck relieved her of the weapon and returned it to his back waistband.

"This is all too much." PJ walked back to the bedroom and stared down at the crib.

Chuck locked the apartment door behind him, making another note to himself to have the locks changed on the apartment and shared bathroom, and to install dead bolts.

"This is insane. Wild Oak Canyon is a tiny little town in the middle of nowhere. It's supposed to be a safe place to raise kids. Now—" she glanced across at Chuck "—I don't feel safe in this apartment, outside…anywhere…" PJ rubbed her arms. "And to think whoever broke into my apartment was in here with Charlie." Her voice cracked. "I can't let anything happen to Charlie. She's everything to me."

The band around Chuck's heart tightened. At one time, he'd thought he was everything to PJ. But that had changed. She'd pushed him away when he'd needed her most. Deployment had been hard enough as it was. But he had felt strongly about giving back to his country, and going to Afghanistan was his way of demonstrating his love for the United States. He had no regrets, other than having been medically discharged when the men he'd fought with remained behind.

He followed PJ into the little bedroom and stood behind her as she stared down at the defenseless baby who couldn't even crawl yet. He knew a feeling of such longing, his chest hurt from it. The tiny baby girl with the short tuft of dark brown hair so like his lay curled on her side, her fist tucked beneath her cheek.

Chuck rested a hand on PJ's shoulder. "I won't let anything happen to Charlie."

PJ leaned into him. "What if you're not here? What if you deploy again? What if an attacker gets to her first?"

"I'm done with the army." The familiar stab of pain in his leg seemed less important than the thought of something awful happening to his baby girl.

PJ stared up at him, her eyes widening. "You're not in the Guard?"

He shook his head, glad for the first time he wasn't deployable. "I'm here now, and I want to be a part of Charlie's life."

PJ leaned her forehead into his chest. "I want to believe you."

"Why shouldn't you?"

"Everyone I ever loved has either died or left me. My mother, my adoptive mother, *you*."

"Me?" He shook his head. "You ended it between us."

"You left for the war."

"I didn't have a choice."

"Point is," her fingers curled into his shirt, "I couldn't take it if something were to happen to Charlie."

"I'd take a bullet for that kid. No one is going to hurt her as long as I'm alive." He wrapped his arms around PJ and added, "And no one is going to hurt you, either. Not if I have anything to do with it."

"Thank you."

Not exactly the response he would have chosen, but it was a start in regaining PJ's trust, as well as learning to trust her. She said she would make sure Charlie was a part of his life. And yet she'd promised to be a part of his. She'd ended their engagement, not the other way around. "You should get some rest."

She leaned away from him and snorted. "Like that's going to happen."

"Do you work tomorrow?"

"Of course."

"Then you need rest so that you don't fall flat on your face waiting tables."

She gave him a weak smile. "I can go without a little sleep. Babies don't always sleep through the night. I had to get used to it."

Guilt ate at Chuck. PJ had been on her own throughout her pregnancy and the first three months of Charlie's life. No one to help her, to let her rest. "I'm here now. You don't need to go two nights in a row without sleep." He rubbed her arms and let his hands fall to his sides. "I'll stay in the living room, in case someone tries to break in again." Chuck backed toward the door. "You'll be okay."

PJ glanced down at Charlie again and then toward her bed. "I can't get over the feeling that my personal space has been violated, that someone is targeting me for some reason." She shivered. "It gives me the creeps. Should I get the sheriff involved?"

"Absolutely."

"In the meantime, I have to live here and I don't feel safe."

"Let me put your mind at rest." He went to the small closet and threw open the door. Inside hung the little bit of clothing that comprised PJ's wardrobe, along with shoes neatly lined up along the floor. "No one hiding in the closet."

PJ's lips quirked. "Scaring away the boogeyman?"

"You bet. Gotta take care of my girls." Chuck bent to look beneath the bed. "Nothing under there but a couple of dust bunnies." He pulled back the clean floral comforter that had seen better days and many washings. "All clear here, as well." He jerked his head to the side. "Get in."

She gave him a lopsided frown. "I'm not a child to be tucked in."

His gaze swept over her from the top of her drying hair to her bare feet, and his groin tightened. "No, you're not. But you've been through a pretty frightening ordeal. It's okay to be scared."

PJ moved toward the bed. "For Charlie."

"For Charlie." With a nod, Chuck shook the comforter, encouraging her to take him up on his offer.

PJ climbed into the bed and pulled the sheets up to her chin. "You'll be in the living room?"

"Unless you want me to stay with you until you go to sleep?" He tucked the comforter around her, his breath held in wait for her answer.

"No," she said, her eyes wide, her fingers clenched around the blanket.

He let go of the breath. What did he expect? She wasn't going to invite him into her bed after one night back. Chuck straightened, fighting back his disappointment and the heat growing inside at the image of PJ's long, silky legs sliding beneath the sheets. He cleared his throat. "Close your eyes and sleep." Then he left, his hand reaching for the doorknob to pull it closed.

"Wait." PJ's voice arrested him in midstep, a hint of fear making it tight.

He didn't turn, afraid he wouldn't be able to leave again if he did. "I'll only be in the living room. Just yell if you need anything."

"I was wrong," she whispered.

Hope blossomed, filling Chuck's chest and lodging with the lump in his throat. Still he refused to face her. "About what?"

"I want you…to stay until I go to sleep." Her voice was little more than a soft sigh. "Please?"

Chuck sucked in a deep breath and slowly turned.

PJ lay against the sheets, her eyes wide, the dark circles beneath them giving her a vulnerable look.

He wanted to tell her no. That he had been wrong to think he could stay with her in her bedroom without holding her, touching her, wanting to kiss her. Inwardly he groaned. "Okay."

She smiled. "Thank you." PJ turned on her side, facing him and the baby crib. "You can sit here." She patted the mattress beside her. "I won't bite."

His teeth grinding in the back of his head, Chuck closed the short distance to her bedside and hesitated. "I'll just stand here."

"I'd never fall asleep with you hovering over me like a vulture." She patted the mattress, her mouth a firm line. "Sit."

Chuck obeyed, sure he was in for the toughest hour of his life. This felt even more dangerous than stalking the streets of an Afghan village searching for insurgents. He settled on the bed, kicked off his boots. Then, resting his back against the headboard, he gave up the fight. "Come here."

PJ scooted closer.

Chuck pulled her into his arms and let her rest her face against his T-shirt. His entire body begged for more. "Go to sleep," he said, his voice gruff.

"You don't have to be grumpy."

"Yes, I do. If I'm not, then I might be tempted to do this." He leaned over and claimed her lips, his own pressing down hard, all the pent-up frustration of having her so close over the past twenty-four hours and not being able to hold her exploding into that one kiss.

Her lips opened on a sigh, her teeth parting, letting his tongue slide in to caress hers in a long, sensuous stroke.

Her fingers climbed up his chest and locked behind his neck, dragging him closer, her breasts pressing against his chest, their bodies melting together.

Chuck's hands slid down her shoulders to the small of her back, pulling her over to lie across him.

His groin tightened, his member pressing into her belly. Nothing but the soft cotton of her nightshirt and shorts between him and...

Who was he kidding? Nothing had changed between them. PJ was working off fear. She didn't want to be alone, and holding him was her only way of feeling safe. He couldn't take advantage of her in her current state.

Chuck gripped PJ's arms and laid her back against her own pillow. "Sleep."

She stared up at him, eyes dark gray-green pools, her lips swollen from his kiss. "What just happened..."

"Shouldn't have. Rest assured, it won't happen again." He tucked the blanket around her and crossed his arms over his chest to keep his hands from straying back toward her.

"Chuck…" PJ cleared her throat.

"Just go to sleep, damn it." He closed his eyes to the vulnerable look in hers. "I'll stay until you do."

She lay still for a long moment, and then the sheets rustled and she shifted.

When Chuck dared to look again, PJ lay on her side, facing away from him, her body rigid. He didn't try to comfort her. Instead he focused on remaining as still as possible.

Before long, her muscles loosened and her breathing grew deeper and steady.

When he was sure she was asleep, he climbed out of the bed. As he passed the crib, Charlie whimpered and rolled to her back, her eyes blinking open.

"Go to sleep, sweetheart," he whispered, smoothing a finger across her velvety cheek.

Her eyes opened wider, and she batted the air with her tiny fists.

Afraid she'd cry, Chuck lifted her into his arms and carried her out into the living room. As soon as he laid her over his shoulder, she gnawed on her fist and settled against him, falling back to sleep.

He gave her a few minutes and then walked back into the bedroom to lay her in the crib. As soon as he tilted her onto her back, her eyes opened and she whimpered again.

Chuck sighed, gathered her in his arms and took her back into the living room. He eased into the rocker recliner and set the chair in motion.

Charlie lay still against his chest. The scent of

baby shampoo filled his senses with a new memory he'd never forget.

This was his little girl, so defenseless and dependent on her parents to protect her from harm. After a while, Chuck stopped rocking and leaned back, lifting the footrest.

Charlie slept on, and before long, so did Chuck.

PJ WOKE IN the darkness, her breasts tight, knowing she needed to rise and feed Charlie. She lay for a moment, listening. Usually Charlie alerted her to the need to eat by crying out. The room was eerily quiet. Too quiet. She tossed the comforter aside and pushed to her feet, crossing to the baby crib.

As she leaned over to check on Charlie, her heart stopped and she almost cried out.

Charlie was gone!

PJ raced out into the living room and almost fell across the outstretched footrest of the recliner.

Chuck's big form lay sprawled across the chair. In his arms Charlie lay sleeping, her cheek resting against his broad chest, a little spot of drool darkening his T-shirt.

PJ froze, her heart seizing, a sob rising to close off her throat.

The big man and the tiny baby looked so right together.

Chuck stirred, his hand touching the baby as if,

even in his sleep, he was checking on her to make sure he didn't drop the precious child.

For a long moment, PJ stared, filling her senses with all of what could have been among her, Chuck and Charlie. With all that had happened, the months of living without him, not telling him about his child and what he'd surely suffered in Afghanistan, PJ didn't know what was best for any of them.

All she knew was what she witnessed. Chuck would make a great father to Charlie. No matter what she'd done in the past, PJ wouldn't stand in the way of Chuck and Charlie's relationship and time together.

Trouble was, where did she fit into the picture? Could she let Chuck back into her life? Would he want to come back? And in what capacity? As the father who has joint custody of his little girl? Or the husband who loves and takes care of his family?

PJ knew very little about Chuck's family. He'd mentioned his parents once to say he was estranged from them, but he hadn't given a reason. What had his childhood been like?

If she and Chuck were to get back together—not that she was leaning in that direction, but if they were—she'd want to know everything. Having Charlie made her even more aware of the importance of family and maintaining that connection.

So many questions were left unanswered and would have to remain unanswered, at least until morning. PJ glanced at the clock on the wall and sighed. She had to be up in three hours to get ready for work.

She gently lifted Charlie from Chuck's chest.

His eyes shot open and he grabbed her wrist, his grip tight enough to bruise. "What are you doing?"

"I'm taking Charlie to feed her." PJ fought not to drop the baby. "You're hurting my wrist."

For a moment, the pressure increased, and then Chuck blinked and looked at her as if for the first time. "PJ?"

"Yes, of course." She glanced at where his hand still held her. "You can let go. I'm one of the good guys."

He jerked back his hand and sat up in the chair. "I'm sorry." Chuck stared at her reddened wrist where he'd held her, his brow furrowing. "Did I do that?"

PJ shifted Charlie into the crook of one arm and shrugged. "It'll be okay."

"No, it won't." He reached out and then stopped, his hand falling to his side. "Maybe it's not such a good idea for me to be here."

"Why?"

"I sometimes have nightmares."

"Post-traumatic stress kind of nightmares?"

He nodded and pushed a hand through his hair. "Yeah."

"I'll take my chances. I'd rather have your nightmares than that nightmare stalking me."

Charlie turned her face into PJ's chest, nuzzling for food. Her fist found its way into her mouth, and she sucked on it with a loud smacking sound.

PJ smiled. "I need to feed Charlie."

Chuck stood and stretched. "Right. I'll just check the doors and windows."

"You've done that already."

"Then I'll do it again." He nodded toward Charlie, sucking PJ's shirt into her mouth. "You better get busy before that one rips a hole in your shirt."

"She's a determined little girl." PJ entered her bedroom, leaving the door open slightly, and turned her back to it before lifting her shirt.

Charlie latched on and settled against her, a hand on her breast, her fingers curling into the skin.

The world stood still while she fed Charlie, leaving PJ with nothing else to do but think. About Charlie, about Chuck, about the way Chuck had kissed her and held her in his arms.

She had no idea what to do next, but she knew she hadn't stopped loving the big man.

Her cell phone vibrated on the nightstand beside her bed, indicating a text message. Who would text her at three-thirty in the morning?

PJ leaned over, careful not to disturb Charlie, and grabbed the phone with her free hand. She clicked on the message from a sender with a blocked number.

The message was long, and for a moment PJ didn't understand. When the words sank in, she dropped the phone and yelled, "Chuck!"

Chapter Seven

When the wind blows, the cradle will rock
When the bow breaks, the cradle will fall
and down will come baby, family and all.

The short bit of a twisted child's lullaby roiled through Chuck's head for the rest of the night, keeping him awake until the gray streaks of dawn crept in around the edges of the curtained windows.

He'd given up on sleep long before dawn and moved around the kitchen, quietly setting out pans and plates for breakfast.

Why would someone target PJ and Charlie and then threaten their family, unless they knew Hank's secret? As soon as he could, Chuck planned to talk to Hank. PJ had a right to know what was going on. Her connection to Hank or to her mother's former fiancé had to be the reason for the threats and attacks.

PJ had to know everything in order to protect herself. And a DNA test would help to prove her lineage and give them a better understanding of what they would be up against.

PJ emerged from the bedroom fully clothed at five-thirty.

Chuck had just cracked an egg into the skillet. "One egg or two?"

"I'm not hungry."

"You, better than anyone else, know that you have to eat." He nodded toward the bedroom. "Charlie's counting on you."

Her shoulders sagged. "I know. One egg."

"Scrambled, right?" He cracked an egg into a coffee mug and stirred it with a fork.

"You remembered."

"There's not much I don't remember about you." He didn't glance up when he spoke. He didn't want to spook her with too much intimacy too soon. Not when he'd almost lost control the night before and kissed her. He'd wanted so much more than just a kiss.

"You like yours sunny-side up." PJ slipped behind him and reached for the glasses in the cabinet next to the sink. She filled them with the last of the orange juice and tossed the jug into the recycle bin.

Hyperaware of her every move, Chuck almost dropped the spatula when PJ pulled open the drawer beside him, her hip rubbing against his.

She grabbed utensils from a drawer, rounded to the other side of the bar and laid them in front of the two bar stools. "Sorry, the apartment isn't big enough for a dining table."

He grinned. "Anything beats eating MREs in the sand."

"How was it...you know...over there?" PJ asked.

Chuck's lips turned downward as a flashback blinded him as effectively as the desert sun. Sand all around, dull, beige-colored hulls of bombed-out buildings in mountain towns. Being alert at all times, never knowing who was friend or foe. Watching every step you took, to avoid improvised explosive devices. Not knowing if a gun would go off in your face around every corner. "Harsh."

PJ swallowed hard. "Why did you come back early?"

He slid the eggs onto the plate so fast, they slipped over the edge and landed on the counter. Chuck slammed the skillet onto the stove and glared across at PJ. "I don't want to talk about it."

PJ held up her hands, her brows rising into her hair. "I'm sorry. But maybe talking about it will help. When you're ready, I'll listen."

Bread popped up in the toaster and Chuck jumped and spun toward the appliance, his fists clenched. When he realized he'd overreacted toward PJ and the toast, he closed his eyes and willed his muscles to relax. "I'm sorry." He turned to face her, plates in hand.

"No problem." PJ's voice was casual, but one

hand rubbed the wrist of the other where light purple bruises were beginning to show.

Chuck set the plates on the bar and took PJ's injured wrist in his hand. "I did that?" He skimmed his thumb over the mark and shook his head. "I'll bed down in the hallway tonight."

"No." Her hands closed around his.

When he tried to pull free, she held on.

"Look at me." PJ squeezed gently.

Chuck gazed into her beautiful gray-green eyes. "I never want to hurt you."

"You didn't. I'm okay, and I want you to stay in the apartment." She sucked in a deep breath and let it out. "I'm afraid for Charlie…and myself. Having you there until this nutcase is caught would help me sleep better."

"Even when I'm capable of this?" He held up her wrist, his jaw tight, lips pressed together.

"Especially because of this. I know you can take care of us better than we could take care of ourselves." She carried his hand to her cheek. "Please. Let it go."

"For now." He pulled his hands free, wanting to take her into his arms and hold her more than he wanted to breathe, but afraid he'd hold her too tight or lose himself again to the images seared into his mind from his deployment.

PJ slipped onto the bar stool and patted the one beside her. "I have to eat in a hurry. Charlie will be awake any moment and demand her breakfast."

Glad for the change of subject, Chuck sat beside PJ as if nothing was wrong. "She seems healthy and happy."

PJ smiled. "Charlie's been an ideal baby from the moment I brought her home from the hospital. Other than the late-night feedings, which is natural for breast-fed babies, she sleeps the rest of the night."

"I want you to put me on the emergency contact list for the day care, in case something comes up and you're not able to pick her up on time."

"I'll do that when I drop her off today."

"And warn the caregivers to keep a close eye on her and keep you informed of any strangers coming in or out of the building for any reason."

PJ set her fork down. "Do you think someone would try to take Charlie?"

"We don't know what the text message meant, but we can't take chances." He would talk with Hank that day and find out if there was anything else he could do to protect Charlie and PJ.

PJ stared at her uneaten egg. "Should I even take her to day care today? I have to work. I can't afford to take time off."

"No. For now, go on, business as usual. Just let the staff know to be aware."

A cry from the other room made PJ jump. "That's my cue." She set her plate in the sink, having taken only one bite of egg and toast.

Chuck didn't like that PJ was so on edge she didn't eat. He'd put security measures in place around the resort and the parking lot where PJ entered and exited the building. And later that day, if they had time, he'd take her out to Hank's and teach her how to fire the Glock.

PJ left at six-thirty. Chuck walked with her to her little car and helped her settle Charlie into the backseat. "I'll follow you to the day care."

"No. It's daylight. I'll be okay for a few blocks. I'm sure Cara Jo has a long list of things for you to do around here today."

"What time will you be done at work?"

"Around three, then I head to the library to use the computer for my online classes."

"Classes?"

She smiled. "Yeah. I started college."

He'd known she'd been saving for it when they'd gotten engaged. "What are you studying?"

"Animal husbandry and business management." Her shoulders straightened, and her eyes glowed with excitement. "I want to work with animals on a ranch or a farm someday."

"I'm happy for you, PJ." His chest swelled. She'd chosen the same field he'd studied. "I'm glad you're getting to realize your dream." And he was. "What time do you pick up Charlie from the day care?"

"Around five. Still daylight. We'll be okay." PJ stood beside her car door, staring up into Chuck's face. "Thanks for being here for us." She leaned up and brushed her lips against his, and then she slid into the driver's seat and pulled away.

Warmth filled Chuck's chest, edging out the cold hollowness he'd experienced in Afghanistan.

PJ had turned onto the main road and disappeared around the edge of the diner, yanking Chuck back to the present. He pulled out his cell phone and hit the speed dial for Hank Derringer.

"Hey, Chuck, I'm glad you called. We need to meet."

Chuck's jaw tightened. "Damn right we do."

"I'm headed into town in about an hour. I'll see you at the diner?"

"Stop by my apartment first. I want to talk to you in private."

"Will do."

Chuck went to work making PJ's home a safer place to live. He installed fresh, brighter light bulbs over the staircase and landing, cleaning the globes of bugs and Texas dust. As soon as he was certain the hardware store would be open, he headed there. On his way past the diner, he slowed long enough to catch a glimpse of PJ through the large windows.

She was busy serving to the morning crowd of cowboys and businessmen and women, her hair pulled back in a ponytail, her face flushed.

Chuck's belly tightened. If anything happened to her...

He mashed his boot to the accelerator and hurried toward the only hardware store in town, hoping it also sold more advanced electronics.

Inside the store, he noted everything a man could

want in the way of nails, screws, plumbing and building supplies. He located new doorknobs with matching locks and keys. Then he went in search of motion-sensing lights.

"May I help you?" An older gentleman stepped up beside him and did a double take. "Chuck?" His eyes widened and he grinned. "Chuck Bolton? Boy, how've you been?" He stuck out his hand and shook Chuck's.

Chuck smiled at the old man. "How are you, Mr. Bergman?"

"Other than rheumatism in my joints and a bum knee, I'm still kickin'. Missed seeing you come in here for supplies for the resort and the stables. Thought you'd left this hole-in-the-wall behind to go into the army?"

"I did for a while when my Guard unit deployed." Chuck clenched his teeth. "Now that I'm back, I'm working for the Wild Oak Canyon Resort again."

It reminded him of his years growing up. When he hadn't been at school, he'd spent all his time outside from the crack of dawn until after sunset, riding, fencing, hauling hay and caring for the animals his father had accumulated over the years.

He could still remember the first horse he'd purchased with the money he'd made helping a neighbor haul hay. There had been some good times, before his falling-out with his father had driven him away and ultimately to this small town.

"Always liked you around here," Mr. Bergman

was saying. "You worked hard and set a good example for the young folk." He clapped Chuck on the back and looked around. "What can I help you find?"

"I need motion-sensing exterior lighting."

"Got some of those in just yesterday and hadn't had time to put 'em on the shelf."

"Grandpa, this cash register is giving me fits." The pretty blonde at the counter slapped the side of an antique register older than her—and probably her parents, too.

"Let me get Ross to help you. He's good with all the electronics and computer gizmos." Mr. Bergman turned toward the back stockroom. "Ross!"

A tall, bulky younger man with a sulky scowl on his forehead appeared in the doorway leading to the rear of the building. "What?"

Mr. Bergman's brow furrowed at the abrupt response. "Chuck here needs some of those motion-sensing lights that came in the shipment yesterday. Help him out while I fix the confounded register."

Ross glared toward Chuck and then turned back into the rear of the building.

"You can go on back and see if they're what you want," Mr. Bergman offered, steering Chuck with a hand on his back. "I'll help as soon as I can."

Chuck followed the surly Ross into the back stockroom.

Stacks of boxes stood in lines, some open, some half-empty and many needing to be unpacked.

"Here." Ross unearthed a black package from inside a cardboard box and tossed it to Chuck.

Chuck caught it, wondering how this boy kept his job. With such a poor attitude and disposition, he would be more of a liability to Mr. Bergman than an asset.

"Well?" Ross stood with his hand on the box full of lighting supplies.

Chuck inspected the outside writing and opened the box to peer inside. "I can use them. I need six."

Ross's eyes narrowed, and a snarl lifted his lip. He grumbled as he dug into the box. "Only have four."

"I'll take them all."

Ross dug the others out, handing them all to Chuck, rather than offering to take them out to the counter.

"Finding what you need?" Mr. Bergman appeared in the doorway.

"Got it," Chuck answered.

"Let me help you with those." Mr. Bergman reached for the black boxes.

"Thanks, but I got 'em."

Ross shuffled around in the back of the storeroom, knocking a box over. "Damn!" The young man shot a killer look at the store owner.

Mr. Bergman led the way out of the stockroom. "That boy has a chip on his shoulder. Would fire him, but he's my only grandson. His mother's divorced and working at the truck stop. She's got enough on her mind without having to worry about her boy."

That explained why the kind old gentleman kept a surly employee on the books.

"I keep hoping he'll find another job. He's been applying, but no takers so far. Ross is a wizard at computers, but he's terrible with people." Mr. Bergman shook his head.

Skills only got you so far, as Chuck had learned. The ability to work with others was vital, a lesson he'd learned the hard way himself. "I'll need new locks and keys, as well."

Mr. Bergman nodded. "I can help you with that."

Chuck paid for the lights and new door locks and left the store. Having been to war with young people who would give their lives for their brothers in arms, he didn't have much patience for people like Ross. He hoped like hell Charlie didn't grow up to marry someone like him.

The thought of Charlie growing up hit him again with the weight of his commitment to the tiny baby. He hurried back to the resort to install the four motion-sensing lights on the corners of the building. Each light and position had its own challenge— from finding electrical wires hidden in the eaves to running the wire out to the corners. Like a puzzle. He'd always enjoyed a good puzzle that he could work out with his brain and his hands. Once he had the wiring in place, he began mounting the lights, aiming the globes at the ground where he knew PJ would be walking.

Now that he was back in Wild Oak Canyon, he had more reason than ever to want to be with PJ. But would it work? She'd ditched him when he'd told her he was deploying. How would she feel about his work for Covert Cowboys, Inc.? The job could prove equally dangerous. With Charlie in the picture, should he give it up and find safer employment? Thoughts whirled around his mind. The clearest one was of Charlie. She needed a father.

While standing at the top of the extension ladder, holding the last light fixture in place with one hand and a screw and screwdriver in the other hand, he fumbled the screw and dropped it.

"Need this?" a deep, accented voice called out from below.

Chuck shot a glance to the bottom of the ladder.

An older, Hispanic man, probably in his sixties, with deeply salted hair, stood on the sidewalk below, holding the screw.

"Yes, I do." Chuck descended until he stood beside the stranger.

The man placed the screw in his hand.

"Thanks."

The man tipped his head. *"De nada."*

"If you will excuse me, I'll finish." A little hesitant to turn his back on anyone, including a mild-mannered older man, Chuck eased up the ladder and twisted the screw in place.

When he glanced down, the man still stared up at him, this time holding the ladder steady.

Chuck descended. "Thank you."

"You're very, how do you say, handy?"

"Comes with the job." He stuck out his hand. "I'm Chuck, the handyman."

The man took his hand in a firm grip. "Ricardo Iglesias. Pleasure."

"Are you a guest here at the resort?"

"Sí."

"From around here?"

"Vacationing from Belize."

Chuck's brows rose. "Vacationing here?" He glanced around at the flat, dry countryside extending out from the back of the resort, more desert than anything else.

The man shrugged. "It has its own beauty and interests."

Chuck understood the man's reasoning. "But isn't Belize a lush tropical paradise?"

"Some would say so. But I believe happiness is derived from closeness to one's *familia*. Regrettably, I don't live close to *mi familia*."

A regret Chuck was all too familiar with. "We all make choices." He'd made his seven years ago.

"Some are made for us, and we must, unfortunately, live with the outcome."

An image of his father rose to Chuck's mind, of the day he'd kicked him out of the house and told him to make his own way in the world. He'd been eighteen. And he hadn't talked to his father since. Nor had he had contact with anyone from his family, including his mother, younger brother and sister, in the seven years since he'd left home.

The older man tipped his head. "Señor Bolton, do you live close to your family?"

"I don't remember giving you my name."

The man shrugged. "I asked in the cafe. Are you close to your family?" he repeated.

The question caught Chuck off guard. His first instinct was to say no, even though his father, mother, sister and brother were less than a hundred miles away. Then he recalled he wasn't alone in Wild Oak Canyon. He had PJ and Charlie. "As a matter of fact, I am." At least Charlie was family. And by default PJ was part of it. Even if she'd chosen to push him away. She couldn't escape the fact that she was Charlie's mother and Charlie was his daughter.

"When you get to be my age, you learn wealth and fame are nothing without family."

"I know that." One look from his baby girl's brown eyes had taught him that.

"You have *niños*—children?" Ricardo asked.

His chest swelled with the love already firmly rooted in his heart for Charlie. "I do."

"Guard them well. Never let them know a day without your love."

"I plan on loving her every day of her life." Chuck glanced at the man, noting the deep lines of sorrow written in his face. "What about you? Do you have children?"

"I do." The older man gave him a sad kind of smile. "And I made many mistakes."

"Is any parent perfect?" Not for the first time, Chuck wondered if he'd be a good father. If the mistakes he made would drive Charlie away as his father's had driven him away.

"Teach your children love and humility through your own example. It's all we can do."

"I'll keep that in mind." Chuck glanced up at the ladder. "If you'll excuse me…"

"*Si,* of course." Ricardo backed away. "I have kept you from your work long enough."

"I hope you enjoy your vacation at Wild Oak Canyon." Chuck collected the empty boxes. When he straightened, Ricardo was gone.

Another glance at the motion-sensing lights had Chuck convinced.

It wasn't enough.

Hank pulled into the parking lot in an older four-wheel drive pickup. The fact that the man had millions, probably billions, hadn't changed what he liked to drive. He parked and climbed down, staring up at the extension ladder still leaning against the side of the two-story resort building.

"Motion-activated?" he asked.

Chuck nodded.

"I take it the attack last night on Danny Reynolds got to you?"

"That and other things."

"Let's go inside, and you can fill me in."

Inside Chuck's apartment, Hank pulled out his cell phone and handed it to Chuck. "Got this text message early this morning."

Chuck read the message, a sick feeling washing over him. "Around three-thirty this morning?"

Hank frowned. "As a matter of fact, yes."

"PJ got the same message."

"Then that's it." Hank dragged in a deep breath, the lines in his forehead deepening. "Whoever is after PJ is probably doing it to get to me. You say he specifically mentioned PJ's father?"

"He said, 'Who's your daddy, little girl?'"

"He has to be someone who knows PJ's lineage."

"Whoever it is has been in her apartment more than once." He told him about the missing monitor and the voice PJ heard. "I'm installing new locks and dead bolts today."

"Good. I'll get my computer guru to set her up with a security system, as well. But it will take time."

"The way things are going, I'm not sure she has time." Chuck stared into Hank's face. "You have to tell her what you know. She deserves to know what she could be up against."

"That puts you in the middle of it. How do you feel about revealing that you've been lying to her about your position here?"

"She won't be happy." She'd probably feel betrayed. Chuck clenched his fist. "What's important at this point is to keep them safe. If telling them about my role in this helps, then so be it."

"When shall we tell her?"

"The sooner the better."

"Bring her and Charlie out to the ranch this evening. We can break it to her then."

"Hank?"

"There's more?"

Chuck handed him the baby monitor he'd wrapped in a brown paper bag. "I need you to use your connections and have the fingerprints lifted off this baby monitor and run it against the Integrated Automated Fingerprint Identification System's database."

"I'll get right on it."

"One other thing." Chuck's jaw firmed. "We need to get PJ's DNA tested."

Hank nodded. "I figured it would come to that."

"Why wait?"

The older man stared out the small window at the sky. "I've already lost one family. If PJ really is my daughter, I couldn't stand to lose her, too."

"And you'd feel differently if she isn't your daughter?"

With a chuckle and wry twist of his lips, Hank answered. "No. I love PJ as if she were my own. But if she's not, someone knows she's connected to me in some way. She could be a target for kidnapping and ransom, either way."

"Or, if her mother's ex-fiancé knows of her existence," Chuck noted, "he could be at the bottom of this and might take her life in revenge for you taking his fiancée."

Hank ran his hand through his shock of gray hair. "And equally as frightening…if he finds out she's his daughter—"

"PJ and Charlie will be in grave danger of kidnapping."

"And taken to Mexico where she might never be found."

Chuck slammed his fist into his palm. "We can't let any of that happen."

"No," Hank agreed. "We can't."

BUSINESS AT THE diner was brisk that morning and stretched right into lunch, giving PJ no time for a break. She wanted to check on where Chuck was. Having him so close and yet not being able to see him…well, it was distracting, tummy-knotting and plain frustrating. Twice she'd ducked into the kitchen to phone the day care. Both times, Dana assured her that Charlie was fine and no strangers had been in or around the facility.

After the attack, the voice on the monitor and the threatening text, PJ couldn't dispel a sense of impending doom, making her twitchy and tightly strung.

Someone dropped a pan in the kitchen and PJ jumped, emitting a tiny scream.

Cara Jo leaned close to her as she passed by with

a heavy tray. "Honey, you're about as nervous as a cat in a room full of rockin' chairs."

PJ pressed a hand to her chest, willing her pulse to slow to normal. "I'm fine."

"Thinking about the attack on Danny last night?"

"Yeah." And the other incidents. And Charlie. And the way she'd felt when Chuck had kissed her.

"I called the hospital this morning. He's going to be fine. They're monitoring him for a concussion one more day, and then they'll release him."

"I'm glad he'll be okay." To think, if Danny hadn't been there, the attacker might have gotten to Chuck or Charlie.

"Why don't you take a break? I'll cover your tables."

"No, but thanks. I need to work. It keeps me from thinking about everything else."

"Including the handsome Chuck Bolton?"

"Is he here?" PJ spun toward the door.

Cara Jo chuckled. "No, but your reaction to his name told me all I needed to know."

Heat burned its way up PJ's neck and into her cheeks. "We're not back together, if that's what you're thinking."

"No?" She raised her brows and smiled. "If the look on your face is any indication, and if the man's still willin', it won't be long."

PJ pressed her palms to her cheeks and made a dash for the ladies' room. Cara Jo was right. She was flushed, her eyes shining and far more animated than they'd been in a long time.

Damn.

She couldn't fall in love with Chuck all over again. She had Charlie, and that was all she needed. Chuck would be like every other adult in her life and either leave her or die. Why get attached only to be left once again?

After a stern jerk on her own bootstraps, PJ washed her hands and emerged from the ladies' room with purpose. A new customer sat at one of her tables, looking around expectantly.

PJ grabbed a menu and went to work. "New to town?" she asked politely.

"*Sí, señorita.* I am staying at the resort for the week." The gray-haired man spoke with a thick Spanish accent, the sound melodic and comforting.

PJ smiled. "You'll like the resort. It's laid-back, and the rooms are all comfortable. Can I get you something to drink?"

"Coffee, *por favor.*"

PJ headed for the coffeepot, snagged a mug and the coffee carafe and returned.

"*Gracias.*" He had a noble air to the way he held his head high, and his piercing brown-black eyes seemed to look right through PJ into her soul.

She shook her head, reminding herself of how little sleep she'd gotten the night before. "What can I get you to eat?"

As she hung the man's order in the window to the

kitchen, a younger man wearing a ball cap entered the diner and sat at the bar, tapping his fingers on the counter until PJ stopped in front of him. "Can I get you something to drink?"

"Coke," he said, his answer so abrupt as to be almost rude.

PJ set the glass in front of him and handed him a menu. "Cara Jo will take your order. She'll only be a moment."

She returned to the Hispanic gentleman, setting out a bundle of cutlery wrapped in a napkin. "Is there anything else I can get you while you're waiting for your order?"

"*Señorita,* are you from around here?"

"Pretty much."

"Can you tell me where I might hire a horse?"

"You said you're staying at the resort?"

"*Sí.*"

"They can arrange for you to ride. They have a stable with several decent riding horses."

"*Gracias.*"

When PJ turned to leave, the man captured her hand. "Pardon me, but you remind me of someone I once knew." He let go.

PJ snorted.

"Do you look like your mother?"

"I don't know. All I have is a faded picture of her. Hard to tell."

The man nodded. "Family means a lot to you?"

Not before. Not when she'd lost everyone she'd

loved. But since Charlie had come into her life…
"It does now."

"As it should."

"Order up!" the cook in the kitchen called out.

When PJ turned to collect the plate, she could see in her peripheral the man at the counter watching her as she crossed the room to the kitchen window.

A chill slipped across her skin.

She had to get a grip. Her paranoia was affecting her work.

If she wasn't mistaken, the young man in the ball cap worked at the hardware store, and he normally walked around with a sullen expression. PJ shrugged and concentrated on her job.

Forty-five minutes later, she grabbed her purse and headed for the library. She'd barely have enough time to finish her homework, load up her new assignments and get across town to pick up Charlie.

While she pulled up her college assignments account on the computer, she checked her email on her smartphone, paging through the spam to get to her instructor's responses to her homework assignments. One email caught her eye, the title blurring as she clicked to open it.

In the subject line, written all in caps, were the words *Rock-a-bye Baby.*

Chapter Eight

Chuck hit the talk button on his cell phone before the first ring ended. "PJ?"

"Meet me at the day care." PJ's voice came across in labored bursts, as if she was running.

"When?"

"Now."

Before he could ask why, the line clicked off. Chuck dropped the ladder he'd been carrying and ran for his truck, leaving a trail of burned rubber on the pavement of the resort parking lot. In less than five minutes, he skidded into the lot in front of the church where PJ had dropped Charlie off the day before.

PJ pulled in behind him.

Chuck leaped out of his truck and joined PJ on the stairs leading up to the door. "What's wrong?"

"Charlie," she said. Without slowing, PJ charged into the church. "We have to get to our baby."

They ran down the long hallway to the entrance and burst through the door.

A woman's scream brought them to a screeching halt.

Dana stood with her hand pressed against her chest and laughed shakily. "You two scared me half to death. What's wrong?"

"Where's Charlie?" PJ demanded, pushing past Dana to move into the room beyond where cribs lined one wall and playpens another. She went straight for the first crib and peered into the bed. "Dear God, where is she?"

"Looking for Charlie?" Another woman's voice called out from the floor at the end of the room, on the other side of a playpen.

"Charlie?" PJ rushed forward.

Chuck followed, his pulse hammering against his ribs.

Lying on her back on a colorful blanket, Charlie stared up at the playset dangling over her. She smiled and kicked her feet.

"Charlie." PJ's voice caught on a sob. "Oh, thank God."

When the baby heard her mother's voice, she turned her head toward her and cooed.

PJ lifted the child into her arms and held her close, tears trickling down her cheeks to splash onto Charlie's silky hair.

"Charlie's okay." Chuck steadied his hand against PJ's back and pulled her into his arms, shocked that he was shaking.

"I was so scared," PJ whispered.

"Do you mind telling me what got you so upset?" Chuck asked.

She pulled her cell phone from the back pocket of her jeans and handed it to him. "Click the link on that email." PJ turned away from him and paced across the room, giving him time to digest what had scared her so badly.

"PJ, what's going on?" Dana stood in the doorway, her face creased in a frown. "Debbie, is everything okay in here?"

The woman who'd been beside Charlie on the floor stood out of range of PJ's pacing. She shrugged. "As far as I know."

Chuck clicked the link and a video came into view, featuring Charlie lying in her crib in the apartment. The video switched to PJ carrying Charlie into the day care. Then another shot showed Charlie sleeping in the day care crib.

As the video ended, dread settled over Chuck's heart like a cold hand. "Which crib is Charlie's?" he demanded.

Dana pointed. "The first one."

Chuck spun and walked to the end of the crib. With his back to the bed, he glanced toward the ceiling at a light fixture, the only object affixed to the textured drywall ceiling. He grabbed a chair, stood on it and unscrewed the glass fixture.

As he pulled it from the ceiling, a tiny black object fell to the ground.

Chuck checked the inside of the globe for any other foreign objects and then replaced it in the fixture and locked it down with the screw.

Careful not to step on the black device, Chuck dropped out of the chair, yanked a tissue from a nearby box and scooped the object from the floor. "It's a remote camera."

PJ, still carrying Charlie close to her chest, appeared at Chuck's side. "Who would do this?"

Chuck faced Dana. "Have any repairmen been in the facility over the past couple days?"

She shook her head. "No one. Everything has been working fine, for once."

"Who has keys to the building besides you ladies?" he asked.

"The preacher and his wife are the only others I know who have keys to this section of the church." Dana glanced at PJ. "I can't believe someone is trying to kidnap my sweet Charlie."

PJ shook her head. "I don't know if someone is planning to take her or if they're just playing some sick joke on me." Her tears had dried, and her gray eyes held a steely glint. "Whoever it is will have to kill me to get to Charlie."

Chuck almost smiled at PJ's determination. If he hadn't been so shaken by the intimacy of the video, he would have. "Come on."

PJ grabbed Charlie's diaper bag and followed Chuck. "Are we going back to the apartment?"

"Only for a moment." Chuck walked toward the infant carriers against the wall and grabbed the one he'd seen PJ carrying earlier. "I'm betting there's another camera just like this in your bedroom."

A shiver shook PJ's body. "Nice to know. Not only is my attacker a child stalker, he's a pervert, as well."

Chuck followed PJ to the apartment and then transferred the infant car seat base to the backseat of his truck. He lifted Charlie out of her carrier and handed her to PJ. "Maybe you should stay in the car."

"If it's all the same to you, I feel safer close to you."

Chuck's chest warmed. Even if PJ couldn't find it in her heart to love him again, at least she felt safe with him. And he felt better knowing where she and Charlie were.

Once inside her apartment, Chuck made a thorough scan of all light fixtures, starting in PJ's bedroom. He found a similar camera mounted to the globe of the ceiling fan aimed at the baby's crib.

"Is this something?" PJ called out from the living room. She'd laid Charlie in her crib and gone back to the living room to help in the search. She squatted on the floor, staring up at the bottom of an end table.

Chuck dropped to his back and stared at the spot she pointed to. A small metal object was stuck under the table with a wad of chewing gum. "Good catch. Got any paper or plastic bags?"

PJ scrambled to her feet and returned a few seconds later with a paper towel and several small paper bags.

Chuck scraped the gum and device from the bottom of the table and into the bag, closing it. "Mark it with the location you found it."

"Gotcha." PJ grabbed a pen from a can on the counter and scribbled on the bag.

After searching every surface, nook and cranny in the small apartment, they concluded they'd found the only devices set.

Chuck left PJ in the apartment and scoured the hallway and the shared bathroom, both efforts revealing nothing more.

When he returned to PJ's apartment, PJ stood with her arms crossed, her face set in tight lines. "What now? Go to the police?"

"We go to Hank Derringer's place."

PJ's arms fell to her sides, her brow furrowing. "Why?"

"He'll explain when we get there."

"Explain what?" She shook her head. "Do you know something I don't?"

Chuck's gut tightened. This was the part he didn't look forward to. "Please, just come with me. Hank can help us with what's going on."

PJ's brows remained dented, her eyes narrowed.

"I'll go, but I sense you're not telling me everything. And frankly I don't like it."

Chuck bit hard on his tongue to keep from retorting.

Before he could say anything, PJ's shoulders slumped and she sighed. "I guess I deserve that, considering I didn't tell you everything about our daughter. I'll get Charlie."

Chuck let go of the air he'd held in his lungs and helped gather Charlie's things.

PJ SAT SIDEWAYS in the front seat of Chuck's pickup, straining at the seat belt to check on Charlie in the back. She seemed so far away.

"Have you ever been out to Hank's place, the Raging Bull Ranch?" Chuck asked.

PJ shook her head. "No. Hank's a nice man and all, but we haven't grown close enough to visit each other's homes."

Chuck nodded. "He's a pretty private man."

"I'd say so. I have the occasional conversation with him at the diner and he seems interested in what goes on around Wild Oak Canyon." PJ stared at Chuck. "How can he help with the situation with Charlie? And why should he?"

"He has resources."

"That's it? That's all you're going to give me?" PJ rolled her eyes and sat back against her seat, crossing her arms over her chest.

When they pulled up to the gate at Raging Bull Ranch, Chuck stopped to press a button.

The speaker above the keypad crackled. "State name and purpose."

"Chuck Bolton. I'm here at Mr. Derringer's request."

In the long pause, PJ noted, "I didn't realize Hank was so well-to-do."

"Not many know." Chuck glanced her way. "He likes it that way."

"Thus the security?"

"Exactly."

The speaker crackled. "Proceed." The gate panels parted at the center, swinging inward toward the ranch driveway.

Chuck shifted into Drive and eased forward.

Halfway open, the gate jerked to a stop. Chuck hit the brake.

PJ pitched forward, caught by her shoulder strap. "What the heck?"

"Probably just a malfunction." Chuck waited, his hand on the gearshift.

The gate lurched and swung toward the truck.

Chuck whipped into Reverse and hit the gas, shooting the truck back as the gate closed completely.

PJ chuckled. "Are you sure Mr. Derringer wants to see us?"

Chuck frowned and punched the button on the keypad.

"State your name and purpose."

"Still Chuck Bolton, and Hank still wants to see us."

"Hmm. Seems to be a malfunction with the gate system. Hold on just a minute, please."

"Can't do much else," Chuck grumbled and glanced across at PJ.

Her brows rose, and she stared at him pointedly. "Since we're delayed indefinitely, why don't you just tell me what's going on?"

"It's not for me to tell." Chuck nodded as the gate swung open again.

"Proceed."

Once again, Chuck eased forward. And again, the gate stopped halfway, lurched and then swung toward them.

A computerized voice blasted over the speaker. *"Ha, ha, ha. Open, close, open, close. Which will it be? Ha, ha, ha."*

PJ gasped. The voice sounded like the mystery voice on the baby monitor when she'd been in the bathroom at her apartment.

"What the hell?" Chuck reversed out of the way of the gate and checked all directions.

"Feeling safe now?" the voice on the speaker wailed.

A black SUV sped toward them from the other side of the fence.

Chuck eased his Glock out of the side pocket of the truck door. "Be ready to duck."

"Why? What's going on?"

"I don't know, but it's never a bad thing to be too cautious."

"I don't like this. Can't we just leave?"

"We need to talk to Hank." Chuck shifted the gun to his left hand and aimed it out the window at the approaching vehicle. "We'll leave if this situation doesn't get better in the next two seconds."

The SUV skidded to a stop. Two men in black jumpsuits leaped from the front, brandishing what looked to PJ like military rifles.

The back door burst open and Hank Derringer dropped to the ground, a frown marring his usually kind face.

From the other side of the vehicle a young, pale-faced man wearing skinny jeans and high-top sneakers jumped down, carrying a pair of wire cutters. "If all else fails, disconnect." He opened a box on the other side of the gate, reached in and snipped wires. He nodded toward the men in black, who pulled the gate open.

Hank walked through and leaned into the driver's window. "Sorry about that. We've been hacked."

"How bad?"

"All the systems have been compromised." He nodded to the man piecing the wiring back together. "Brandon Pendley is my tech support. He'll have us up and running soon. Mind if I ride back to the house with you?"

"I'll ride in back with Charlie." PJ slipped out of the front seat and dropped to the ground before Chuck could protest.

"Thanks." Hank held the door for PJ and then climbed into the front passenger seat with Chuck.

Chuck pulled through the open gate and along the winding, paved road through a stand of scrub oak trees.

"PJ, has Chuck told you anything about what's going on?" Hank asked.

PJ's lips tightened. "Not a thing. And frankly, it's pissing me off."

Hank chuckled, cleared his throat and shot a glance over the back of the seat. "Blame me. I asked him not to."

"Why would you ask him not to tell me anything? What would a handyman know that's so all-fired important?" PJ shook her head, and then her heart skittered a few beats, anger shoving her pulse into high gear. "Unless Chuck isn't really a handyman at all. What the hell's going on?"

The truck burst through the last stand of oaks into a clearing graced by a large, sprawling ranch house built of white limestone and cedar.

"Come in out of the heat, and I'll tell you everything." Hank hopped down and opened PJ's door for her.

"Darn right you will. Then Chuck and I are going

to have words." She glared at Chuck's reflection in the rearview mirror.

Chuck unlatched the infant carrier from the base and carried it, Charlie and all, into Hank's house.

PJ followed, stepping into the wide foyer with its high ceilings and smooth, Saltillo tiles. Though large and sprawling, there was nothing ostentatious about the beautiful home.

The warm terra-cotta-colored walls and Mexican tile floors invited her in. Had she visited under any other circumstances, PJ would have enjoyed exploring the rooms with the Southwestern decor and sturdy leather furniture capturing both the grace and beauty of the desert view through the windows.

"Come into my study." Hank led the way.

PJ followed the older man into a large room with floor-to-ceiling bookcases filled with leather-bound volumes, hardback fiction and well-worn paperback novels.

A large desk sat in the middle of the room, the wood an unusual light shade and pattern. She'd seen a table like it in the antique shop in town. Mr. White, the owner, had told her it was mesquite and handcrafted in a small town in Texas.

Hank strode to the desk and stood there, leaning back against the fine wood. He waved to the bomber-jacket brown leather couch. "Please, have a seat."

Chuck set the infant carrier on a cushion in the middle of the sofa.

PJ perched on the edge and peered down at her daughter, still a little shaky after the scare of the video.

Charlie stirred, her eyes blinking open.

PJ unbuckled the restraints and lifted the baby into her arms, and then glanced at Chuck.

Chuck remained standing near the end of the couch, his feet spread, his arms crossed over his chest, his gaze on Hank.

Dragging in a deep, fortifying breath, PJ turned and gave Hank her full attention. "What's going on?"

Hank sighed. "We're not exactly sure. But I think someone might be targeting you and Charlie to get to me."

PJ's arms tightened around her baby. "Why?"

"It's a long story." Hank shoved a hand through his shock of graying hair.

PJ leveled her gaze on the man. "I'm listening."

Hank told her a story about Alana Rodriguez, a beautiful woman he'd met in Cozumel, Mexico, and how she'd been on the run from her abusive fiancé. He went on to tell PJ about how he'd helped her hide until he could arrange for her to relocate to the United States. He gave her the money, the tickets and a new identity so that she could start fresh, free from fear of her fiancé ever finding her.

"What happened to her?" PJ asked.

"She made me promise not to contact her when I returned to the States. She said her fiancé had many connections on both sides of the border and they were dangerous. And it was just as well I didn't contact her." Hank turned toward the window. "As she'd suspected, Alana's fiancé learned of my connection to her and sent his thugs to…extract her whereabouts from me. I told them I didn't know what they were talking about." Hank snorted. "That didn't stop them from breaking my nose and two ribs. When they couldn't get anything out of me, her fiancé paid off the local Mexican police and had them arrest me for her murder."

PJ's heart hurt for the older man standing in front of her. She could almost feel the pain of his injuries, the fear of giving up even a shred of information that would seal the beautiful Alana's fate. "But you didn't kill her."

He turned to face PJ. "If I told the officials that she was still alive, her fiancé would have continued looking for her."

PJ leaned forward. "What did you do?"

"Spent time in a Mexican jail, hired half a dozen attorneys and finally was released six months later."

"How did you get off the charges?"

"They never found any concrete evidence a murder had been committed. No body. No blood. No crime." He laughed, the sound anything but amused. "I hopped a plane for Houston and never returned to Cozumel. I didn't dare contact Alana in case her fiancé traced her through me. He had connections."

"I don't understand." PJ shook her head. "What does that have to do with me?"

"I didn't know when I sent her away that she was pregnant, and I couldn't contact her to let her know what had happened. I'd made a promise. Based on what happened in Cozumel, I couldn't contact her without risking her life. I didn't hear from Alana again. I didn't even know she'd died until years after her death."

"How did you find out she'd died?"

"I received a letter from an attorney upon the death of the woman who'd adopted Alana's baby."

PJ's gut wrenched, and tears slipped from the corners of her eyes. A knot the size of a baseball lodged in her throat. She couldn't say anything, couldn't tell Hank not to tell the rest of the story. As if standing in the path of a train, PJ couldn't move, couldn't leap to safety.

"Alana had left a letter to be delivered to me should anything ever happen to Terri Franks—"

"My adoptive mother." The tears fell, dripping onto the baby in PJ's arms. "I'm Alana's daughter."

Chapter Nine

Chuck leaned forward and touched PJ's arm. He wanted to hold her, make the hurt and uncertainty go away, but she needed to hear Hank out. "Let me take Charlie." He smiled, aiming for reassurance. "Please, before you soak her."

PJ stared down at Charlie as if seeing her for the first time. Teardrops stained the baby's outfit, and a few had landed on her face. "I'm sorry, sweetheart." She brushed them away and gave up, handing her to Chuck. She turned back to Hank. "Is that the meaning of the voice on the monitor? When he asked...*who's your daddy?*" Her voice dropped to a whisper. "Do you know who my father is? Is he Alana's abusive fiancé?" Her gaze went to Charlie. "I'll kill anyone who tries to hurt my baby."

Hank shook his head. "That's just it—we don't know who your father is without a DNA paternity test."

Chuck braced himself for the next revelation.

PJ frowned. "Is there any doubt the monster is my father?" When Hank didn't answer immediately, PJ's eyes widened. "Did you have an affair with Alana?"

Hank nodded. "She hid in my bungalow for days. She was beautiful, I was young...I fell in love with her."

"And you sent her away." PJ stood and paced across the room, her gaze shooting to Charlie. "How could you love her and never contact her again?"

"I made a promise to Alana."

"All this time I wondered what my father was like. My mother told me he'd died before I was born. I imagined him to be a kind man and that he'd have been a good daddy, had he lived." PJ stared across at Hank. "I never dreamed he could have been a killer, a member of the Mexican Mafia." Her eyes were narrowed, and her jaw tightened. "Or potentially a deadbeat who didn't even bother to check on the woman he professed to love."

Chuck winced at PJ's attack on his boss.

Hank nodded. "I deserved that."

PJ faced Chuck, her frown deepening. "And you."

Chuck stiffened.

"How long have you known all this?" PJ demanded.

"Not much longer than you."

"You knew when you moved into the apartment next to mine, didn't you?"

"Not until the next day. I only knew I had a job to protect one of Cara Jo's employees. Not who, or why."

PJ stared at him as if he'd grown two heads.

Chuck's heart twisted. This was not how he'd hoped the meeting with Hank would go. But PJ had to know.

"You weren't hired to be a handyman?"

He shook his head, absorbing her glare and wishing he could ease the blows PJ was taking.

She held out her hands, her lips pressed together. "Let me have my baby."

Chuck laid Charlie in her arms, wondering if he'd ever be allowed to see his daughter again.

Anger sparked from PJ's moist eyes. "I feel like I've been living in lies of other people's making. No one is who they said they were. Even my mother lied to me." She turned to Hank. "The least you can do is give me a ride back to my apartment."

Hank's brows dipped. "It's not a good idea."

"And it's a good idea to stay here with a man who abandoned the woman he loved and didn't even bother to know she had a child?" PJ shook her head. "I could be your daughter." She tipped her head back and closed her eyes. "God, I've been a fool. You're the unknown benefactor. You gave me the scholarship to go to college."

"PJ, I'm sorry." Hank walked toward her, hands outstretched. "I should have told you. I don't know why I didn't. I guess I was afraid if I did, it would put you at risk of Alana's fiancé coming back to find you. I've kept tabs on his movements over the years. His power within the cartel has grown. He's been responsible for hundreds of murders and kidnappings." Hank stopped in front of her, his hands falling to his sides. "I've lost one family. Now that I've found you, I couldn't lose you, too."

"Hank." She said his name like a curse. "You never had me. You don't even know if I'm your daughter without a DNA test." PJ turned toward Chuck. "Please. Take me home."

Chuck shook his head. "Not until Hank sends a team in to check for more bugs. I'm not sure it's safe for you and Charlie to stay there anymore."

"I'm not staying here. Not with a man who professes to care about family, but only a select few. And another who's been lying to me since he returned. I've had it. The only person who hasn't lied to me is Charlie."

The baby stirred in her arms as if sensing her mother's unhappiness.

PJ pressed a kiss to her daughter's forehead. "Take me back to Wild Oak Canyon. I'll go to the sheriff. Let them protect me. I don't need you or your bodyguards."

"PJ, the sheriff's department wouldn't know what they're up against. They barely have enough resources to handle local crime." Hank sighed. "Let me send a team in. I promise I'll get you home once they've cleared the apartment. In the meantime, my housekeeper has prepared a meal for us."

"I'm not hungry." PJ's stomach rumbled, belying her statement.

Chuck hated seeing PJ so hurt. The woman had gone through so much, and there wasn't an end in sight. But they both had someone else to keep in mind. "Eat for Charlie."

PJ bit down on her lip.

Chuck could tell she wanted to tell them both where to go. His lips twitched at the stubborn set to her jaw. PJ was a strong woman, and she'd do what was right by her daughter.

Finally she sighed. "For Charlie."

THE MEAL STARTED off in silence. Which was just fine by PJ. Enough had been said for a lifetime. And the sooner she left this house the better. Her heart felt bruised, and she was tired beyond her usual exhaustion from working at the diner. The roller coaster of emotions she'd experienced over the past forty-eight hours had taken their toll, and she didn't know how much more she could bear.

Hank sat at the head of the table with PJ on one side, Chuck on the other and Charlie in her infant seat, balanced on a chair beside PJ.

The housekeeper had prepared a roasted chicken so tender the meat practically fell off the bone. Hank passed the different dishes to her and Chuck, playing the gracious host. Genetically, they could all be related. By outward appearances, they were one big happy family.

PJ almost laughed out loud at the word *family*. Did anyone know what a family was anymore?

For that matter, she'd known Chuck for three years and he'd rarely mentioned his family. PJ assumed his parents were dead. But then what did she know? Apparently not much. Everyone who'd ever professed to love her had kept her in the dark about all the important stuff. She didn't know who to believe anymore.

After choking down several bites of the savory meal, PJ decided she'd go for more answers. "Chuck, in all the time we've known each other, you've never mentioned your family." She stared across the table at him. "Are they still alive?"

Chuck sat for a long time, his fork poised over his plate, his gaze on the food.

He paused so long, PJ thought he'd either forgotten the question or had chosen to ignore it.

Finally, he spoke. "They're alive."

PJ sucked in a breath, feeling as if she'd been punched in the gut yet again. She nodded. "And here I thought Charlie had no other relatives in the world." The lid burst on PJ's emotions, and she shoved back from the table so fast, her chair toppled over backward. "Please excuse me. I need to go throw up." She grabbed Charlie's carrier and darted from the room.

Not knowing where to go, she ran to the opposite end of the house, ducking into an open door and finding a beautiful sitting room with an antique Victorian sofa, a dainty rocking chair and a fireplace with a beautifully carved mahogany mantel. The

room was so different from the rest of the house, PJ
had to wonder who it belonged to until she noticed
the portrait over the mantel.

Hank Derringer, with silver-streaked hair, sat beside a beautiful, raven-haired woman who held a
baby in her arms. Hank and the woman smiled, appearing to be happy.

She remembered seeing them at the diner, looking happy and in love. When news got out that she
and the toddler had disappeared, she'd volunteered
to help search for them. Her heart pinched at the
devastation she'd witnessed in Hank's face back
then. Having her own baby to protect, PJ couldn't
imagine the grief Hank had lived with.

PJ set the carrier on the floor and sank to her
knees, the pain in her chest so great, she found it
difficult to breathe.

Charlie whimpered.

"I know, baby. Grown-ups are so messed up."
PJ lifted her daughter into her arms and the baby
nuzzled her, searching for the comfort of her
mother's breast.

PJ lifted her shirt, shifting Charlie close.

The baby latched on, making smacking, sucking
noises as she settled in.

The love she had for her daughter swelled in her
heart, overwhelming her with emotion. For so long,
PJ thought she and Charlie were alone in the world.
In the past few hours, she had learned that not only
were they not alone, but they had extended family,

the grandparents PJ missed growing up. And no one had bothered telling her until now, when their whole world had gone to hell.

A movement at the door jerked PJ out of her musings, and she glared at the intruder.

Chuck leaned against the door frame, a scowl etched into his brow and his mouth pressed into a thin line.

"If you don't mind, I'm feeding Charlie." PJ shifted so that her bared breast was out of view of the big man. "Is a little privacy too much to ask for?"

Chuck shook his head. "We need to talk."

"Can't it wait?" PJ shut her eyes, blocking out the way the light caught the highlights in Chuck's hair and emphasized the dark circles beneath his eyes. He'd aged in the time he'd been away. What had happened to him in Afghanistan?

PJ told herself not to care, but damn it, she did. "So is the only reason you're hanging around us because you're being paid to by Hank?"

"No." He entered the room and pulled up a wingbacked chair to sit across from PJ. "After I discovered it was you, I thought about going to Hank and telling him I didn't want the job. But knowing you and Charlie were in danger, I couldn't."

"Nice to know you had a moment of hesitation." PJ hated that her voice sounded waspish. She wanted to be the one to rise above the craziness with grace and dignity, to set a good example for her daughter.

Yet anger still burned in her belly, along with the desire she couldn't force away.

Sex had never been an issue between the two of them. Honesty and trust had. The way things were going more recently proved nothing had changed.

"Since I'm pretty much a captive audience and you don't appear to be taking my plea of privacy seriously…" PJ glared at Chuck. "What do you want?"

"I want you to understand."

"That you lied to me?"

Chuck's brows rose, his gaze slipping to the baby contentedly nursing.

PJ sighed. "Okay, I guess we're even."

"Not by far." A muscle in Chuck's jaw twitched. "I've missed three months of my daughter's life."

With a nod, PJ gave it to him. "Touché." She glanced up at him. "Why have you never mentioned your family until now?"

"I don't talk to them. Haven't for seven years."

"Why?"

"It doesn't matter." He stood and paced away from her, stopping to stare out the window.

"If you ever want me to trust you again, you can start by trusting me with whatever deep, dark secret you're holding on to regarding your family." She tipped her head. "Is one of them a murderer?"

Chuck shook his head. "No."

"Then how bad can it be?"

"Let's just say I refused to live up to my father's

expectations." He stood with his back to her, his body rigid.

PJ wanted to go to him, but she had to remain still while Charlie nursed. She decided it was just as well. Being mad at Chuck had easier consequences to deal with than falling in love with him all over again.

"My father was a colonel in the army. He retired when I was ten and moved to West Texas, bought a ranch and raised us to take care of the animals, like they were our troops."

"That doesn't sound so bad."

"The man never forgot his military connections and wanted his sons to follow in his footsteps."

"You went into the army. Isn't that following in his footsteps?"

"He doesn't know that."

PJ frowned. "Why?"

"My father wanted me to accept a football scholarship to West Point."

"And you didn't?"

Chuck shook his head. "I accepted a scholarship to Texas Tech, no ROTC, no military."

"Your father wasn't happy, I take it."

Chuck faced PJ. "My father was so angry, he called me a coward. He told me to get the hell out of his house and don't bother coming back. That was seven years ago."

"We met three years ago."

"I'd finished college, got a degree in animal husbandry with a minor in financial planning. When I graduated, I didn't know what I wanted to do. I got a job as an assistant manager of the resort here in Wild Oak Canyon because it was close to the area I'd been raised, and I could be around the animals."

He dropped into a chair and ran a hand through his hair. "One day I met a man who was vacationing in the area. He'd been to Afghanistan. He told me stories about his platoon, about the tough living conditions and the dangers they faced on a daily basis."

PJ snorted. "So you signed up for the army?"

"Not then. It wasn't until he told me how he wished he could go back and help. He'd give his life for his brothers in arms." Chuck looked up at PJ. "I wanted to feel that commitment. I wanted to know what it was like to care that much about the people around you. To love them like family should love each other.

"Before we met, I'd joined the Army National Guard unit he'd been attached to and went to basic training. When I got back I was in a holding pattern until the unit came back in rotation to deploy. I picked up where I'd left off here in Wild Oak Canyon, but with the training I'd received, I didn't feel like I belonged. I felt like I still hadn't done my part, shown my patriotism."

"But then you met me." The pain etched in his face made PJ's chest tighten. "Were your father's words still playing in the back of your mind?"

"Yes." Chuck dragged in a deep breath and let it

out. "I wanted to know what it was like to face death and want to charge right back into it."

"You wanted to prove to yourself you weren't a coward."

"In Afghanistan, I saw things…faced death…" He bowed his head. "I know now. Family is everything."

"Then why haven't you reconciled with them?"

He glanced away. "I got kicked out of the army."

"Why? What happened?"

"I lost it."

PJ sat up, switched Charlie to the other breast and asked, "What do you mean?"

"There was a kid who hung around outside the wire. Whenever we left the compound to go out on patrol, he was there. He always had a smile for us, and we brought him candy and gum."

Chuck's voice thickened. "One day when we left on patrol, he wasn't standing by the gate waiting for us. Instead, there had been a pile of rags where he usually waited."

PJ closed her eyes to the immediate flood of tears. "The boy?"

"The Taliban had beaten him to death and thrown his body out there for us to find and to serve as a reminder to the other children of the village not to side with the Americans."

"What happened?"

"I'd never felt such rage. When people talk about seeing red, that's what I saw. The red of the boy's blood smeared over his ragged clothing. The red of all the bloodshed that continued in a region that had never known a time of peace." Chuck stared across the room, his gaze far away. "I wanted to crush the people who'd done that to the boy, to their country, to the innocent lives they took on a daily basis."

PJ breathed in and out, and then asked in a whisper, "What did you do?"

"I went into the village against my CO's orders." Chuck's face hardened, and his eyes narrowed. "I went alone to where I'd heard the Taliban had been hiding out." Chuck's fists clenched so tightly, his knuckles turned white.

PJ's heart pounded as she waited for him to continue.

"I killed them. Every last one of them."

She touched his arm, her chest hurting, feeling some of the pain Chuck must have felt to have placed his own life at risk to seek revenge for an innocent boy's death.

Chuck stood, shrugged and walked away. "I went against orders. They were planning to stage an attack later that night. I didn't know about it. I went ahead of their plans. I could have ruined the mission."

"Instead, you risked one man's life over your unit's lives." PJ shook her head. "You could have been killed."

"What they did to that kid…" He stopped again at the window. "I couldn't get the image out of my head. I got shot in the leg and barely made it back to camp."

PJ gasped. "I didn't know you'd been injured. Is that why you limp?"

Chuck nodded. "My CO was pissed. Because of my wound, I was evacuated from Afghanistan. The doctor wouldn't allow me to return. It didn't matter. Even if I could have, my CO probably wouldn't have let me."

PJ ached for Chuck, for the horrors he'd seen and endured. "You lived."

Chuck snorted. "Some life. I barely slept, and when I did, I woke up fighting. The psych doc called it PTSD. With my leg messed up and a lousy psych eval, the doctor recommended a medical discharge. My CO agreed."

"Did you *want* to come home?" PJ asked, bracing herself for the answer.

Chuck shook his head. "Even though I knew you were back here, I didn't want to leave my buddies behind to fight on without me." Chuck stared down at his hands. "I wasn't given a choice." He squared his shoulders and faced her. "Now you know all my darkest secrets."

PJ stared at the man, so hardened, a little lost—so different from the one who'd left a year ago. Yet he was still the same man she'd fallen in love with, the man who was kind to animals and little children. "Why haven't you been back to see your parents?"

"I lived up to my father's expectations. Having failed the military, I've failed him. I couldn't go back."

"Seven years is a long time to go without speaking to your parents."

"It doesn't matter." He straightened. "The important thing to consider is how to keep you and Charlie safe from whoever is stalking you."

PJ couldn't let it go. "You have a daughter, Chuck. Doesn't she deserve to know who her grandparents are?"

"If they refuse to accept her because of me, she's better off not knowing."

"A lot of time has passed. Don't you think your father will have changed his mind? What about your mother?" PJ glanced down at Charlie, her heart squeezing as she imagined a child of hers never coming back to visit. "Don't you think she should have a say in this? What about siblings? Does Charlie have aunts and uncles?"

For a moment Chuck was silent, his eyes sadder than she'd ever known them to be. "Yes, an uncle and an aunt."

Charlie finished feeding. PJ straightened her shirt and lifted the baby to her shoulder, patting her back gently. Over her daughter's little form she stared at Chuck.

"Personally, I think you're being selfish." She stood so that she could look at him, eye to eye.

"It's been too long." Chuck's face steeled. "Let it lie."

The past few days had brought it home to PJ that it wasn't right to hold back. Not when it came to family.

"No." PJ walked right up to him. "I barely knew my mother. Never had a father, grandparents or siblings. If Charlie has a chance at family, by God, I'm going to see that she gets it."

"And I'm here to see that you live long enough to stand on your damned soapbox. Then you can have what you wanted, and I'll get the hell out of your life. But I'll always be a part of Charlie's." Chuck stormed from the room.

"You may be out of my life, Chuck Bolton, but you'll never be out of my heart," PJ whispered.

Chapter Ten

Dusk had settled into darkness as Chuck marched through Hank's house. When Hank waved him into the study, he almost told him to go to hell.

Then he reminded himself he wasn't mad at Hank. He was mad at himself for letting PJ's words get to him. For letting his father's rejection taint his life for seven long years. And for the painful reminder of the family he missed so much it hurt.

Some of the tension seeped out as he entered Hank's private domain.

The older man didn't waste time. "Just heard from the guys checking out PJ's apartment."

A lump of cold, hard lead settled into Chuck's gut. "What did they find?"

Hank stopped behind his desk. "You don't want PJ to go back tonight."

"That bad?"

"Someone broke into her apartment and tossed it." Hank pulled a bottle of whiskey off the counter behind his desk, grabbed a couple of shot glasses and held them up. "Care for some?"

Chuck shook his head. He hadn't had a drink since he'd returned to Wild Oak Canyon. As much as he craved one to steady his nerves, he had to keep a clear head. Charlie and PJ needed that much from him. "I had just changed the locks on the doors."

Hank's eyes narrowed. "As far as the guys reported, it didn't look like forced entry. Whoever got in picked the lock or had a key."

"Why would they toss the place?"

"I don't know. There weren't any messages left behind. PJ would have to tell us if anything was missing." Hank set the bottle back on the counter unopened. "Point is, it's not safe for her to return to the apartment."

Chuck dragged in a deep breath and let it out slowly. "And you want me to break it to her?"

Hank shook his head. "I'll do it."

"You might want to." A wry smile tugged at Chuck's lips. "She's not too happy with me right now."

"I'll see what I can do to smooth her feathers."

"Good luck. She doesn't take kindly to feather-smoothing." Chuck nodded toward the computer on Hank's desk. "Your guy Pendley find the hacker yet?"

"He's still working on it. He has to go back to a week-old recovery backup. Once he has it installed and the new firewall program in place, he'll work on finding the hacker. Right now he's just trying to keep the bastard out of my bank accounts."

"Seems like he has a bone to pick with you. Doesn't sound like the work of a Mexican Mafia man. Don't they usually go for more guerrilla tactics like chopping off heads and drive-by shootings?"

"I have to admit, these attacks don't make much sense. The only connection they have to me is PJ and Charlie."

"Your Achilles' heel?" Chuck offered. "They were an easy target as long as they were outside your perimeter."

"My perimeter has been breached via the computer. I don't know what help I'm going to be other than providing firepower to a game of cat and mouse."

"Think back. Have you made anyone angry lately? Anyone who might have the ability to hack into a computer system as effectively as he has?"

Hank's eyes narrowed. "Not recently. Brandon's been working for me for the past eight months. He's been busy putting firewalls in place and beefing up the equipment and software it takes to run this place and my financial holdings. He also helped me set up the database for the Covert Cowboys, Inc. Thank goodness the hacker hasn't broken into that one."

"Brandon's done all that in only eight months?"

Hank smiled. "The kid's amazing. Possibly the best technical support a man could hire."

"Did you interview other candidates before you hired him?"

"We're talking eight months ago. Surely whoever is causing trouble now hasn't been stewing for eight months."

"Some people carry grudges a long time." Chuck didn't add, *like my father.* For that matter, Chuck had been carrying one around since the day he'd left home and never looked back.

He could still see an image of his mother through his rearview mirror as he'd driven away in his beat-up truck. She'd been standing on the porch, his teen-age brother Jake's arm around her shoulders, his ten-year-old sister, Katie, running after his truck, crying.

Not a day went by that he didn't think of them. And his father hadn't even stepped out of the house—refusing to see his son off as he left home for the last time.

Katie would be seventeen now. Chuck wondered if Jake had gone to West Point as his father had wanted his boys to do.

Chuck had to get outside. He needed to burn off steam and memories before he exploded.

"Chuck?" Hank's voice cut into Chuck's musings. "You still with me?"

"Not really." He scrubbed a hand across his face. "I have too much on my mind. Is it possible for me to borrow a horse?"

"Going for a ride this late?"

"If I can. I have to get some air."

Hank nodded. "Supposed to be a clear night with

a full moon. Should be bright enough to see most anything. My foreman can fix you up."

"Thanks." Chuck headed for the door.

"In the meantime, I'll inform PJ of the break-in. And Chuck, what are the chances of getting PJ to agree to a DNA test?"

Chuck paused at the door. "Somewhere between hell freezing over and a snowball's chance in hell."

Hank sighed. "Either way the test turns out, I feel like she's part of my family, and I wouldn't want anything bad to happen to her or Charlie."

"You and me both."

"Again, no matter what, it puts her at risk for kidnapping. If she's Alana's ex-fiancé's daughter, he's possessive. He'll want her and Charlie with him in Mexico. If she's mine, he might still want me to suffer for taking Alana away from him, and pay me back in kind by taking PJ and Charlie away from me."

"I understand." Chuck's shoulders straightened. "No one's taking PJ or Charlie away. They'll have to go through me first."

"And me."

Chuck nodded. "Then we're in agreement."

"One hundred percent." Hank's lips lifted in a hint of a smile. "Go ride. I'll keep an eye out for PJ and Charlie."

Chuck left the house and strode to the barn.

A light shone inside. Apparently, true to his word, Hank had called his foreman, giving him the heads-up. The man had led a black gelding out of a stall and was settling a saddle blanket on his back.

The smell of hay, sweet feed and the earthy scent of horse manure filled Chuck's head with memories. "I can do that," he offered.

"Been around horses much?" the foreman asked.

"Since I was ten."

The older man tipped his head in the direction of a door. "Bridles are in the tack room. Saddles are on the rack."

Chuck saddled the horse, adjusted the stirrups for his long legs and led the animal out of the barn into the big, Texas night sky.

Already he could feel the worries melting away from his shoulders. Not that he'd forget about Charlie and PJ. Not when they weighed heavily on his mind. But the other stuff he'd revealed to PJ could blow away with a strong Southern breeze for all he cared.

For seven years, he'd pushed his family to the back of his mind. Seven years he'd tried to forget the look in his mother's eyes and the way Katie ran after him. It all came crashing back on him with the harsh look on his father's face as he'd told him to leave.

Chuck led the gelding to the nearest gate, which opened into the huge pastures stretching out and away from the ranch house. Once through, he latched the gate and stepped up into the stirrup, swinging his leg over the saddle.

The gelding didn't need any encouragement. As if he, too, had a few cobwebs to clear, he lurched into a gallop, flying across the flat land, dodging sage and prickly pear cactus.

Chuck bent low over the gelding's neck, the wind in his face fresh, scented with yucca and dust.

For a long stretch, he gave the horse his head, letting the animal set the pace. When he finally settled into a steady trot, Chuck reined him to the west, riding toward the property line that bordered the highway. If he kept going, they'd run into the fence. He wanted to check the front gate to see if they'd fixed it or if it was still jerking open and closed.

The huge, arched gate rose out of the darkness, standing higher than any scrub brush in the pasture.

Chuck slowed the gelding to a stop, tied him to a fence post and walked the rest of the way to the rock and wrought-iron gate. When he reached it, he breathed a sigh. The gate was closed. Whether or not the mechanics worked was another question. At least he could rest a little more easily knowing someone wasn't just going to drive right in and wreak havoc on the ranch house and its occupants.

He'd turned and was headed back to the horse when the gelding whinnied.

An engine sound buzzed along the highway at a distance, moving closer, coming from the direction of Wild Oak Canyon.

Chuck glanced over his shoulder toward the sound, but he didn't see any headlights. The noise grew louder, and still no headlights appeared in the distance.

He untied the gelding and led him into the moon shadows beside the rock gate and stroked his nose.

After a moment, a motorcycle pulled up to the gate, lights out. The rider, dressed in black, wore a black helmet with a dark visor pulled down over his face. He stared at the closed gate for a minute and then laughed, spun the bike around and raced back the way he'd come, lights still off.

Chuck jumped out into the road, hoping to read the license plate numbers on the back of the bike. The rider had obviously disengaged the taillights and he'd removed the license, if there'd ever been one.

A mile down the road, the headlights blinked on.

If there hadn't been a fence in the way, Chuck might have followed on horseback, but the motorcycle would have quickly outpaced the already tired gelding.

Chuck rode back to the barn, eager to check on PJ and Charlie. But first he had to report what he'd seen at the front gate.

Hank wasn't in his study. Chuck found one of the bodyguards.

"Where's Hank?"

"Follow me." The bodyguard led the way to a door that opened to a staircase, leading into a basement below the house.

The walls were solid concrete, as was the ceiling overhead. For all intents and purposes, it was a bunker.

The bodyguard stopped at a steel door and bent to a machine next to it, pressing his thumb on a pad and then leaning close.

A retinal scanner scanned his eye, and a lock clicked. The door opened and they entered.

"Ah, Chuck, back so soon from your ride?" Hank stood next to the young man who'd dismantled the gate earlier.

The man sat hunched over a computer keyboard, his gaze intent on the screen where page after page of numbers and letters scrolled by in rapid succession.

"Chuck, I don't believe you've been properly introduced to our computer expert, Brandon Pendley."

The man at the keyboard raised his hand without turning around. "Nice to meet you," he said.

"Likewise."

"You'll have to excuse Brandon. He's in the process of reloading a backup of our system software. Ever since the computer was compromised, he's been fighting to get us back online."

"Any luck isolating the hacker?"

"Not yet," Brandon said. "I made a ghost copy of the system on a separate backup server, hoping to fool the hacker into thinking we're still infected. When I get us back up and running, I'll go after him and nail the guy."

Hank crossed his arms. "Brandon has taken this attack personally."

"He hacked the corporate computer," Brandon said. "How could I not?"

"Hank, do you know anyone who rides a black motorcycle?" Chuck asked.

"I have one, not that I ride often. Otherwise I can't think of anyone I know personally. Why?"

Chuck told him of the rider who'd stopped at the gate and drove off without headlights.

"Think he's our hacker or maybe the man who attacked PJ?" Hank asked.

"Maybe. We don't even know if they're one and the same." Chuck didn't like not knowing. "Any word on the baby monitor?"

Hank nodded. "We were able to lift prints, but so far my contact in Austin says there are no matches in the IAFIS system."

"So maybe this is our guy's first crime," Chuck suggested.

"Or he's never been caught."

"Tomorrow I'll escort PJ to the apartment and have her look around for anything that might be missing."

"Good idea."

Chuck glanced around at the concrete walls. "Quite a place you got here."

Hank shrugged. "A man never knows when he might need a bomb shelter. I can't say that I've led a pristine life, and my wealth makes me a target."

"Any news on your wife and son?"

Hank shook his head. "Nothing over the past two years except a cryptic hint from that corrupt FBI agent who died in the operation Zach Adams handled for us."

"Any clues as to who in the FBI he was talking about?"

"No. And no leads on my family."

"I won't let anyone take PJ and Charlie."

"What scares me is that I had security in place and he managed to get to them."

Chuck's fists tightened. "I'm not going to let that happen again."

"How did your talk with her go?"

"Great." He glanced away.

"I guess you don't want to talk about it." Hank yawned and stretched. "Better get some rest. I have a feeling things are going to get worse before they get better."

Chuck nodded and headed for the door leading out of the bunkerlike basement. Once in the main part of the house, he went in search of PJ, anxious to make certain she was still there. With all that had happened, he didn't trust anyone else with her safety.

Chuck paused outside the door to the bedroom Hank had assigned to her. He'd even brought his son's crib in for Charlie.

He tapped softly but got no response. When he pressed his ear to the door, he couldn't hear movement inside. Chuck tried the handle, but the door was locked.

While frustrated that he couldn't get a visual on the two women in his life, he understood PJ's wariness. She had to be scared to death for Charlie.

Chuck moved on to the room Hank had offered to him next door to PJ and Charlie. At least he was close enough to help if the need arose.

Still too wound up to sleep, Chuck opened the French doors and stepped out on the porch, inhaling the warm, dry night air. Insect songs filled the sky with a constant hum. The temperature had fallen at least twenty degrees since sunset to a comfortable low seventies. A full moon outshone the stars, creating an almost dusky glow.

A movement caught his attention, and he turned.

PJ leaned against the rock exterior of the house, wearing a soft white nightgown. On PJ it was loose and flowing with the little bit of night breeze lifting the hem to expose her long, lithe legs.

Chuck's pulse increased. God, she was beautiful. The moon, still low on the horizon, bathed her half in light and half in the shadows of the house, giving her an ethereal blue glow.

"Can't sleep?" she asked, her voice little more than a whisper.

Chuck heard her over the sound of the cicadas. "Sleep is overrated."

PJ chuckled. "I try to tell myself that, but it doesn't help when I'm in the seventh hour of my shift at the diner." She stepped toward the porch railing and tipped her head back, closing her eyes. "I love the night in the country. It seems so peaceful, like nothing bad could happen when the stars are twinkling and the land is at peace."

When she'd moved forward, the moonlight shone through the nightgown, silhouetting her body through the sheer white fabric.

Chuck's breath caught and held.

"Didn't you grow up on a ranch?" she asked.

Swallowing hard past his rising desire, Chuck answered, "We didn't move out onto the ranch until I was about ten, when my father retired from the army."

"Do you miss it?"

He stared out at the night, the shape of the barn and the outlying pastures bathed in a gentle glow. "Yes." He'd loved the life of a rancher from the moment they'd moved into the old ranch house.

His mother had made the house a home, filling it with colorful curtains and pillows and the smell of fresh bread baking in the oven.

He turned away from the scene in front of him. "That's no longer my life."

"But it could be…if you wanted it."

"Can't really make a living ranching unless you have a spread as big as the Raging Bull Ranch and money to seed the livestock."

PJ nodded. She'd served enough ranchers at the diner to know ranching was a hard way to make a living. Many had gone under and sold their spreads to commercial ranchers or big game outfitters. Still, if someone had a dream… "Everyone has to start somewhere."

"And where is that starting point for you?" Chuck moved closer and leaned against the railing. "What do you want out of life, Peggy?"

PJ sucked in a breath, remembering how she'd loved it when he'd used her full name. Chuck had been the only person to call her Peggy since her mother had died. Even her adoptive mother hadn't called her Peggy except on the few occasions she'd been angry. PJ shook herself and tried to focus on Chuck's question, not her heart beating out of control at his nearness. "I'm past my starting point." She lifted her chin and gazed up at him. "I'm well on my way to the life I want."

"Are you?" He cupped her cheek, smoothing a strand of hair behind her ear. "Just you and Charlie?"

"We're the only people I can count on." She hated that her voice quavered or that she liked the feel of his work-roughened fingers on her skin. Despite her vow not to, she leaned into his palm.

"What about me?" he asked.

She swallowed hard. "You left."

"I'm back." His lips descended, hovering over hers, his breath warm against her mouth.

"How do I know you won't leave again?"

"The only guarantee in life is death." He brushed

his thumb over her lips. "Is that what you want? A guarantee?"

"Yes," she said, tears pooling in her eyes.

"You will never get those. And in the meantime, you'll miss out on all life has to offer, risks included." His mouth swept across hers, his tongue pressing between her teeth to find hers.

PJ melted against him, too tired to resist, too emotionally drained by all that had happened to care about the consequences or to rouse her earlier anger. She needed his kiss, his embrace, like a drooping flower needed rain.

His tongue stroked hers in a long, sensual glide as his hands smoothed down her back. His fingers slid over her buttocks and cupped the back of her thighs, and he lifted her, wrapping her legs around his waist.

Her sex pressed against the ridge beneath his jeans, sending sparks of awareness racing across her nerves. PJ laced her fingers behind his neck and dragged him closer still, the tips of her breasts rubbing against the cotton fabric of her nightgown, the friction making her nipples bud and tighten.

Chuck leaned her against the limestone wall of the house, the warm ridges pressing into her back.

When one of his big hands slid beneath the hem of her gown, PJ was powerless to resist. She wanted to be naked with him, to feel his skin against hers.

Her fingers slipped between their bodies, attacking the buttons on his denim shirt, flicking them free in rapid succession.

Chuck lifted her and carried her through the open French doors into her room, kicking the door shut behind him. He sat her on the edge of the bed, grabbed the hem of the gown and whipped it up over her head.

Her arms free, PJ pushed the shirt over his shoulders and down his back. She tugged the tails from his waistband, and the shirt fell to the floor.

Chuck's fingers went to his belt.

PJ stopped him with a hand over his and a short shake of her head. "Let me."

He lifted his hands to her face, cupping them around her cheeks. "You're even more beautiful than the day I left for deployment."

She snorted softly, unbuckled his belt and slid it through his belt loops. Then she pushed the rivet through the buttonhole on his jeans and slipped the zipper down, freeing his member into her hands. "Remember the last time we visited the swimming hole at Sandy Creek?" PJ wrapped her hands around his shaft.

His sucked in a breath, his head tipping back. "All too well."

"That was the day Charlie was conceived."

"You know that for sure?" he said, his voice more strained with each stroke of her fingers.

She had always liked that power over him. She had him in the palm of her hand with a few simple strokes. Too bad it hadn't changed his mind about going to war. Now that he was back, she could barely remember why she'd been so angry. "Don't you remember what you said?" She glanced up, her gaze meeting his in the light from the moon shining through the window. "I was trying to convince you not to leave."

"I had to. I had a commitment."

"After we made love, you said it was magic and that you'd never forget."

"I never did." His fingers threaded through her hair. "And that magic conceived Charlie?"

She smiled and shrugged. "I like to think so." Then she let go of a low chuckle. "That, and I counted the days from my last period. I would have been ovulating at that time." She rubbed her cheek against the velvety skin of his member. "I like the other story better."

Chuck's fingers slipped lower, and he hooked her beneath her arms and laid her back against the quilted comforter. Then he shucked his jeans and lay down beside her in all his naked, masculine glory. "Every time with you was magic."

For a moment PJ pushed aside all the old hurt, the fear and the sorrow of losing him. She wanted to feel the power of their connection, to put aside the hollowness of her existence since he'd been gone. "Show me some of that magic tonight."

"Are you sure?" His brows furrowed. "What about tomorrow?"

"You said it yourself." She touched her hand to his face. "No guarantees."

"That's not what I meant." His lips brushed across her eyelids, one then the other. He held her face with his hand as he bent to kiss her, taking her lips with such gentle firmness.

PJ shifted his hand from her face down her throat to her breast and lower. "This is what I have to offer." She guided him to the apex of her thighs. "Tonight."

"Does this mean you're not mad at me anymore?"

"I was afraid of losing you." PJ kissed him, her knees parting, allowing his hand to cup her.

He parted her folds, his finger finding the tender nubbin between and flicking it until she gasped. He slipped a finger into her, swirling around her moist channel, and then another, stretching her entrance.

PJ dug her heels into the mattress, her hips rising to meet his thrusts, a moan rising up her throat.

"Please," she begged, urging his body over hers.

He slipped between her legs, his member pressing into her, filling her.

PJ closed her eyes and gave herself up to his magic.

Lost in the beauty of the moment, she didn't stop to think about tomorrow. She lived for the moment, every muscle, nerve and blood cell reveling in the present, the bombardment of sensations and the explosion of her senses.

When she finally fell back to earth, she lay spent in his arms, a happy glow warming her from the inside.

Chuck gathered her into his arms and pressed a soft kiss to her forehead. "You know, this changes everything."

PJ rolled into his side, pressing her face against his chest, refusing to acknowledge anything past the moment. There would be time later to sort through her feelings. Tomorrow would come all too soon.

Chapter Eleven

Something moved in the darkness, jerking Chuck out of the first deep, dreamless sleep he'd had in a long time. He sat up straight, straining to find the source of the noise.

A silhouette disengaged from the corner shadow and stepped into the predawn light edging through the windows of the French doors.

Chuck slipped silently from the bed and moved toward the form, grabbing it around the middle and clamping an arm around its throat. "What the hell are you doing?" he demanded.

"Trying to breathe," said a raspy female voice.

It was then that Chuck's mind cleared the remainders of sleep and he realized just who was sneaking around the interior of the bedroom. His arm loosened. "PJ?"

"Yes, you idiot. Who else would it be?" She rubbed at her throat and faced him, fully dressed in the clothes she'd worn the day before. "I have to go to work in an hour, and I need to stop by my apartment for a change of clothes."

Chuck stood in front of her, naked, shoving a hand through his hair and trying to focus on what she'd said when all he wanted was to toss her back in the bed and make love all over again. "You can't go to work. It's too dangerous."

She planted a fist on one hip. "I have to go to work. It's how I make money to pay for Charlie's diapers."

"I'll buy her diapers."

PJ's eyes narrowed. "I'd rather do it. Besides, it takes more than diapers to raise a child. I can't stop working or quit school because one person is making my life hell."

"The contacts are becoming more frequent and personal. Who knows what this lunatic will do next?"

"Last night you said life isn't full of guarantees. I can't put my life on hold waiting for something that may never happen."

"What about Charlie?"

"I'm going to set up a playpen in the office at the diner so that I can keep an eye on her. Between me, Cara Jo and the cook, we'll all keep her safe."

"I don't like it."

"You don't have to. It's my life."

Her words hit him square in the gut. "And I'm not a part of it? Is that what you're saying?"

"I didn't say that. I just don't know how you fit in it yet." She slipped into her shoes and stared across at him. "I can get one of Hank's bodyguards to take me to town."

"Like hell you will."

"Then you'll have to put some clothes on. I don't think the Wild Oak Canyon police would condone public indecency."

"Give me a minute to shower and dress."

"I'll give you ten. It'll take at least that long to feed Charlie."

As if aware she was being talked about, the baby squirmed in her crib and let out a pathetic cry.

"That's my cue." PJ scooped Charlie up in her arms and sat on the side of the bed, pulled up her shirt and guided the baby to her nipple.

No matter how many times Chuck witnessed this natural connection between PJ and Charlie, he couldn't help but marvel at the miracle of life.

"Nine minutes," PJ stated, her brows raised.

Chuck gathered his clothing from the floor and hurried into the bathroom connected to PJ's bedroom.

He shot a glance over his shoulder as he stepped through.

PJ was watching his every step.

A smile curled his lips as he twisted the handles on the water faucet and stepped beneath the spray. The cooler the water the better, if he planned to wear jeans in five minutes or less.

A quick shower cleared the remaining vestiges of sleep from his head and chilled the lingering desire from his body. He dressed quickly and ran a hand over his stubbled chin. Shaving would have to wait until he could get back to his gear in his apartment. He feared if he took too long in the bathroom, PJ would pull a dumb stunt like finding someone else to take her into town.

When he emerged into the bedroom, PJ and Charlie were gone.

"Damn woman," Chuck muttered. "Couldn't wait a lousy ten minutes." He dragged his boots on and hurried down the hall to the front of the big house. But when he heard voices in the kitchen, he made a sharp left.

Standing at the counter, stirring a spoon in a mug, PJ was smiling and talking to an older woman Chuck recognized as Hank's housekeeper.

"You can pour that into this insulated cup if you like and take it with you," she was saying. She set a disposable cup on the counter beside PJ.

"Thanks, I will." PJ tipped what smelled like hot tea into the white cup and set the mug in the sink. When she turned and spotted Chuck, a smile lifted the corners of her lips. "Want a cup of coffee to go?"

"That would be great."

"I'll fix it if you'll change the baby's diaper. Or vice versa."

"I'll take a chance on changing Charlie, if she'll take a chance on me." He lifted Charlie from her carrier and blew a raspberry against her belly.

Charlie giggled and grabbed a fistful of hair.

"Hey, slugger, I believe that belongs to me." He pried her fingers loose and settled her in his arms.

"I think there's a diaper left in the bag, and a changing mat, as well." As she pulled a mug from a cabinet, PJ nodded over her shoulder toward the bag on the chair beside Charlie. "You can take her into the sitting room."

Chuck hadn't changed a diaper since his baby sister had come home from the hospital when he'd been eight years old. Surely it couldn't be any harder now than it had been then. With the improvements they'd made to disposable diapers, how could he go wrong?

Five minutes later, with the diaper tape stuck to his fingers and a squirming Charlie refusing to lie still, Chuck was about to give up and call for reinforcements.

"Here, let me help." PJ knelt on the carpet beside them and held on to Charlie's ankles while Chuck repositioned the diaper beneath her bottom. Before PJ could settle her daughter against the diaper, it curled upward, as it had a dozen times before.

"I don't get it."

"The trick is not to worry." She laid the baby down on the curled diaper and pulled the edges out to the side, straightening it before tugging the tapes across the middle. "See? Nothing to it."

"I'd have gotten it sooner or later." Chuck didn't like that he'd failed at his first attempt at changing Charlie's diaper, but he was a quick learner and he'd get it right the next time. Right then all he could think about was how good PJ smelled beside him. Her hair held the scent of honeysuckle on a warm summer day, and her cheeks glowed a soft pink this morning, the glow that had been missing the day before.

Before she could scoop Charlie up and stand, Chuck captured her face in his hands and kissed her soundly, and then he let her go.

She laughed. "What was that for?"

"Rescuing me and Charlie from a fate worse than death."

"A little melodramatic, maybe?"

"A twisted diaper is nothing to laugh about." He lifted Charlie into the crook of his arm and pushed to his feet, a stab of pain reminding him of his injured leg. He offered his free hand to PJ.

She took it and let him pull her to her feet. "Ready?"

He winked. "For anything you have in mind."

Her brow furrowed. "Work. I'm going to be late if we don't get going."

"Hear that, Charlie? We're making your mama late." Chuck carried her to the truck. After PJ settled the infant carrier into the base, Chuck buckled Charlie in.

The drive to town went by in comfortable silence, with the sun rising to the east, spreading a warm, golden glow across the horizon. The weatherman had promised a scorcher that day, but for now, it was tolerable and pretty outside.

If they could nab their troublemaker, all would be pretty darn right with the world.

Chuck parked in back of the resort. "Wait for me and we'll go up together."

PJ stood beside the truck as Chuck retrieved Charlie. He handed her to PJ and led the way up to PJ's apartment.

"Let me go first." Chuck moved ahead, testing the doorknob. It was locked. Hank's men who'd checked it out the night before must have locked it behind them. Chuck fit PJ's key into the lock. It turned easily, and he pushed the door open.

PJ leaned around him and gasped, her face pale. "Wow."

The place was in shambles. Whoever had been inside had turned every drawer upside down, emptying the contents onto the floor. Sofa cushions had been tossed, and clothing was strewn about the bedroom.

"I'd have no idea what was taken, if anything, until I set the place to rights." PJ tried to step around Chuck.

He held his hand out. "Let me." Picking his way across the floor, he inspected the little apartment, looking for anyone still lurking in the closet or under the bed. Then he searched for hidden cameras in case whoever had been inside had hidden fresh devices throughout. When he was as satisfied as he could be without picking everything apart, he nodded to PJ. "You can come in."

PJ handed Charlie to Chuck and moved about the apartment setting chairs on their feet, putting drawers back in the kitchen cabinets and finally making her way into the bedroom for clothing.

She picked up a pair of jeans and dropped them into a basket. "I don't even want to wear any of these clothes until they've been washed." For a long moment she stared at the mess, her face tight and bleak. "I'll wear what I have on until after work when I can get this stuff to a Laundromat. At least I have a clean uniform waiting for me at work."

"Off the top of your head, is anything missing?"

PJ stood in one spot in her bedroom and turned in a 360-degree circle. Facing the bed, she stopped. "The photograph that was on my nightstand." She darted forward and checked the ground beside and under the bed, tossing clothing to the side as she searched. "It's not here." She stood and worked her way through the living room, tossing pillows, sheets, towels and anything else in the way of her search. On her hands and knees, she crawled around the room until she stopped in front of the bookshelf. "Oh, my God." She knelt beside the case and stared at the books scattered across the floor.

"What?" Chuck moved forward with Charlie, whose eyes were wide and curious.

"My photo album. The picture in the frame and the photo album were all I had left of my mother.

All the photos are gone." She pressed her fist to her mouth, blinking back tears.

Chuck held out his hand.

She stared at it for a moment, swallowing convulsively. "That's it. I have nothing left of her."

"You have Charlie." He bent and took her hand, pulling her to her feet and into the curve of his arm, opposite Charlie.

When Charlie saw her mother, she smiled and leaned toward her, arms outstretched.

PJ took her, rested her cheek against the baby's and leaned into Chuck's chest. "Those things were all I had of my childhood with my mother."

"We'll make new memories. You can fill albums full of pictures of Charlie growing up."

"Why is this happening to me?" She let Chuck hold her for a long time.

He wanted to beat to a pulp whoever had been in PJ's apartment and taken the things she'd held dear. For now all he could do was hold PJ and let her grieve again for the mother she'd lost. The more he thought about PJ and her mother, the more it reminded him of his own mother, and he missed her more than ever.

After a few moments, PJ straightened and wiped the moisture from her eyes with the back of her hand. "I have to go to work."

"Cara Jo would understand if you called in sick."

"I need to stay busy. If I sat around and thought about everything, I'd go crazy."

"What can I help you do?"

"Carry the playpen to the office in the diner." She glanced around at the box of diapers. "At least he didn't destroy Charlie's things."

While Chuck folded the portable playpen, PJ gathered diapers and a change of clothing for Charlie. When she started awkwardly picking up the scattered clothing while holding Charlie, Chuck caught her hand.

"I'll come back in a little while and do that. You worry about Charlie."

He'd return as soon as PJ was settled in at the diner. "Are you sure you don't want me to take care of Charlie today? You'll be busy waiting tables."

"Cara Jo won't mind. She usually spends part of the day going through paperwork in the office. She'll keep an eye on Charlie and let me know if she needs anything."

"I don't like the idea that you might have to leave her unattended. Leave her with me. I promise to take good care of her."

PJ glanced up at Chuck, her brows pulled low. "Are you sure you can handle her? I could take her to the day care…"

"No, I'd feel better knowing exactly where she is. Until this insanity is over, I'd feel better if she's with either you or me at all times."

"Okay." She sucked in a deep breath. "I guess we won't need to move the playpen downstairs."

"No, I'll need it here, while I gather your clothes for the Laundromat."

"Maybe I should call in sick. You shouldn't have to pick up my clothes and things."

"Stop worrying." Chuck gripped her arms and stared down into her eyes. "I wouldn't offer if I didn't want to help. Besides, it gives me some one-on-one time with my girl." He held out his hands.

Charlie leaned into them, and PJ let her go to Chuck.

"See?" Chuck grinned. "She agrees. We'll have fun hanging out in the apartment and running errands."

"You'll let me know where you're going?" PJ leaned forward and kissed Charlie.

"Charlie might not, but I will." His eyes narrowed. "Now get to work, woman."

"I'm going." PJ gave one last glance around the room. "I'll be glad when life gets back to normal."

"I've been waiting for that for a long time." Chuck tilted his head. "Sometimes we just have to adjust to a new normal."

"Well, if you're taking care of Charlie today, you'll need to know a few things." PJ showed him where the frozen breast milk was and how to defrost it without making it too hot for the baby to drink.

"Does Charlie eat solid foods yet?" Chuck asked.

"Not yet. I'm still nursing, and she gets all the nutrients she needs for now. I'll start introducing cereals soon."

Chuck had forgotten how complicated raising a baby was. His mother had handled most of that for his sister. He'd just been responsible for an occasional feeding and diaper change. But how hard could it be? Charlie wasn't even mobile yet.

"Okay, then. I'm off." PJ headed for the door.

Chuck followed. "We'll walk you over. I can get breakfast there, and then we'll come back and tackle the apartment."

"Thanks, Chuck." PJ leaned up on her toes and pressed a kiss to his cheek.

He turned at the last minute, capturing her lips with his own. Unwilling to end the brief exchange, he wrapped his free hand around her waist and pulled her closer.

Charlie cooed and fisted a hand in PJ's hair.

When she pulled back, PJ winced. "Hey, that's mine." She pried Charlie's fingers loose, kissed them and descended the stairs.

Chuck locked the door behind him and pocketed the key.

In the diner, PJ went right to work, slipping into her uniform and apron. Then she grabbed a pot of coffee and started her rounds of filling cups.

The diner was busy with the early morning customers stopping for a quick bite before heading off to work.

"Thank goodness you're here." Cara Jo swished by, carrying a tray filled with steaming plates of eggs and pancakes. "I thought I could handle them all without your help if you didn't make it in, but I was wrong."

"I didn't stay in the apartment last night."

"Oh?" Cara Jo's brows rose, and her gaze shifted to where Chuck and Charlie were sliding into a booth.

PJ wished she could take back her words. She'd rather have stayed silent than to have stirred up a barrage of questions. "Forget I said anything."

"Hardly." Cara Jo winked. "You can fill me in after the rush."

"Or I can just work and keep my mouth shut," PJ muttered as she hurried forward to take Chuck's order.

"I heard that," Cara Jo said. "You're not getting off that easy."

As busy as they were at the diner, PJ didn't have time to dwell on the fact that Chuck seemed to be handling Charlie just fine. Seeing him with her daughter made her only more aware of him as a man, as a father and as someone who would be a permanent part of Charlie's life.

How that would work out in the long run, PJ had no idea. With an attacker on the loose wreaking havoc in her life, she didn't want to look past the current situation to think about what might lie in her and Charlie's future.

When Chuck finished breakfast and left with Charlie, PJ found herself wishing she could have gone with them. Instead she threw herself into her work, waiting tables and cleaning up after customers.

By the time two o'clock rolled around, she was tired and thankfully had worked off the worry of the night before.

"I have some things to check on at the resort office. I'll be right back. Don't go anywhere until we've had a chance to talk." Cara Jo left through the front door of the diner.

Seeing a chance to escape before Cara Jo returned, PJ slipped off her apron, ran for the back room and changed into her street clothes. On her way out the back door of the kitchen, she remembered she hadn't taken out the trash, her last task of each day. PJ grabbed the two large garbage bags and hauled them toward the back door.

"Leave those, and I'll get them when I'm done cleaning the kitchen." Mrs. Kinsley stood with her hands up to the elbows in sudsy sink water.

"It's okay, Mrs. K. I'm on my way out anyway." PJ left the diner through the back door, weighed down by the two bags. She stopped several times to reposition her hands on the bags before she made it to the Dumpster. Once she had the bags dealt with, she'd round the side of the building and make a quick stop in her apartment to check on Charlie and Chuck before going to the library to do her homework.

PJ practically fell backward lifting the first bag up over the edge, but she finally managed to roll it into the bin. When she had the second bag perched on the edge and ready for a final push in, black plastic slipped down over her head, obliterating the bright sunlight.

At first she thought she'd dropped the trash bag on her face. But when she breathed in to cry out, the bag filled her mouth, cutting off any chance of air.

PJ let go of the trash bag she'd been balancing and it slipped away, crashing in front of the bin. Before she could pull the plastic bag off her face, her hands were captured, wrenched behind her back and tied together with a hard plastic tie.

She struggled, fighting with all her might as someone dragged her by her arms several feet and dumped her on the ground, and then tied her ankles together with the same hard plastic line.

The more she fought for air, the deeper the loose plastic filled her mouth—until the world faded and she could struggle no more.

In the haze of semiconsciousness, PJ lay on her side, wrists and ankles bound. The heavy weight of a knee pressed into her side and kept her pinned to the gravel. The bag was pulled from her mouth but tied tightly over her eyes before she could catch a glimpse of sunshine.

With her mouth wide open, PJ sucked in a deep breath.

Hands pulled her head back and jerked her jaw downward. A stick was jammed into her mouth, and something cottony scraped across the inside of her cheek. Then the stick was removed and the weight lifted from her side, the hands let go of her face and footsteps pounded away from her.

For a long moment PJ lay on the ground, breathing to desperately fill her starved lungs. The only sound she could hear was the rustle of the plastic bag over her eyes and ears and the rattle of her breaths. The sun beat down on her, so hot she could feel her skin beginning to burn. She knew she should shout to let someone know she was there, but she just didn't have the strength.

"Help," she cried, her mouth dry, her voice croaking. "Please."

Chapter Twelve

Chuck and Charlie had spent the morning talking to the Wild Oak Canyon police about the break-in. They'd come, taken pictures and promised to catch PJ when she got off work for additional comments to add to their report.

After they'd done what they could, Chuck and Charlie spent the rest of the morning rearranging PJ's apartment. Or at least Chuck had done the work—Charlie had lain in the playpen, watching his every move until her eyes drifted closed and she napped.

Besides the missing photos and a few broken mugs tossed from the cabinet, there had been little damage. Chuck gathered the clothing strewn across the floor and dumped it into a pillowcase and the laundry basket. He'd hauled it down to his truck, fitted Charlie in her carrier, left a message at the diner for PJ that he was leaving with the baby and where he was going, and made the short drive to the only Laundromat in town. There he'd spent a couple of hours feeding quarters into the machines and sorting darks and lights.

Charlie talked to him with little cooing sounds, smiled and batted at him with her little fists, keeping him thoroughly entertained. The more he was around his tiny daughter, the more she wrapped him around her little finger. Chuck couldn't imagine another day in his life without Charlie in it. He was falling in love with her so fast it scared him. He prayed PJ wouldn't change her mind about letting him see his little girl, that she wouldn't sue for sole custody, thus taking away both of the girls he loved.

After folding the laundry, Chuck piled it all into his truck. On the way back to the apartment, Chuck stopped at Wild Oak Canyon Hospital to check on Danny's status.

The nurse said he was awake, preparing to leave as soon as the doctor released him. Chuck and Charlie could go in for a visit.

Chuck knocked on Danny's door.

"Come in," a voice called out.

Danny sat on the edge of the hospital bed, a big white swath of bandage wrapped around his forehead. He wore jeans, a T-shirt and tennis shoes and appeared to be anxious to leave as soon as the doctor gave him the go-ahead.

Alicia stood beside the bed, her purse slung over her shoulder, her hand in his. They both turned toward the door as Chuck entered carrying Charlie.

"Hey, baby girl." Alicia smiled at the baby and then turned a more serious expression toward Chuck. "Mr. Bolton, thanks for stopping by to check on Danny. I don't know what I would have done the other night if you and PJ hadn't been home."

Danny held out his hand. "I hear I owe you a thank-you."

Chuck took his hand and shook it. "I didn't do much. Just stood by your side until the real heroes showed up. The med techs did all the work."

"Well, thanks for being there for me and Alicia." Danny shook his head. "I hate to think what might have happened if I hadn't been meeting Alicia that night. That guy was on his way to Ms. PJ's apartment."

"Do you remember anything about the guy?"

"I gave the police my statement. I didn't see anything. The man was wearing a ski mask. As soon as he saw me, he came after me with the tire iron. I didn't have a chance to get away."

"Can you remember if he was tall, short, fat or thin?"

Danny closed his eyes. "When he was standing on the stairs above me, he seemed taller, but as he got to the bottom, he wasn't quite as tall as I'd originally thought." Danny shrugged and opened his eyes. "Not much to go on."

"Any distinguishing features? Tattoos, rings, voice?"

"No rings that I remember, or tattoos for that

matter. And he didn't say anything. Sorry, I'm not much help."

"Thanks anyway. If you think of anything later, don't hesitate to let me know. Sometimes even the smallest detail can be important."

"I'll let you know."

"In the meantime, meet your girlfriend in a well-lit area from now on." Chuck smiled at them and left. Without a description, Chuck had nothing to go on. He returned to the apartment and unloaded Charlie and the laundry.

PJ usually got off work at two o'clock. As the hour came and went, Charlie fell asleep and Chuck paced.

By two-thirty, he'd waited all he could stand. As much as he hated waking Charlie, he needed to check on PJ. She'd said something about going to the library but had promised to stop by the apartment before she left.

Charlie stirred a little when he lifted her out of the playpen and onto his shoulder, where she fell back to sleep with little effort.

He locked the door and descended the steps. PJ's car sat in the parking lot where they'd left it the night before. Chuck figured she was working late to make up the time she'd missed earlier.

Chuck and Charlie rounded the front of the resort complex to enter the diner.

Cara Jo met him at the door. "Hi, Chuck. The diner's closed until four. Can I do something for you?"

"I was looking for PJ."

"Mrs. K says she left thirty minutes ago."

Chuck frowned. "She didn't stop by the apartment like she said she would, and her car is still here."

"Maybe she was late for her class and got a ride with someone."

"It's online. I didn't think she had to be there at a certain time. And she promised to stop by the apartment before she went to the library."

Cara Jo's brows dipped. "That's not like her to ditch someone." She strode to the kitchen door. "Mrs. K, what time did you say PJ left?"

"Right after two." Mrs. K wiped her hands on her apron and rounded the big butcher block in the middle of the kitchen, where she'd been rolling out dough for biscuits. "She took the trash as she left through the back door. I told her I would, but she insisted."

"Can you hold Charlie?" Chuck shoved the baby at Cara Jo.

"Sure." Cara Jo took Charlie and laid her over her shoulder.

Chuck ran out the back door and stood in the gravel, his gaze panning the lot behind the diner. No sign of PJ, but a bag of trash lay on the ground in front of the bin, split open with the contents spilling out onto the ground.

Chuck's heart leaped to his throat. He sprinted to the trash container and peered inside, half expecting to see PJ's crumpled body lying among the cardboard boxes and bags of trash. He breathed a sigh when all he saw was more trash and no PJ. Had someone kidnapped her without leaving a trace?

Chuck spun, his pulse racing, his hands clenched into tight fists. He didn't have a clue where to look. "PJ?" he called out, desperate.

A low moan sounded from behind the trash container.

Hope surged, sending Chuck flying around the side of the big metal Dumpster.

Lying on her side, her wrists and ankles bound with zip ties, her head half covered in a black trash bag, lay PJ.

Rage and worry blasted through him as Chuck dropped to his knees beside PJ and yanked the bag from her head.

She cringed, her eyes closing tightly and then opening in short blinks. "Chuck?"

"It's me, baby."

"Where's Charlie? Is she all right?" Her voice was raspy.

"She's fine, sweetheart." He pulled his knife from his pocket and sliced through the bindings at her wrist. "Cara Jo is holding her."

Her hands free, PJ rolled to her back and rubbed at the raw stripes on her wrists. "How long have I been out here?"

"About thirty minutes." He sliced through the zip

tie on her ankles and folded his knife, shoving it into his pocket. "Did your attacker hit you?"

"No, but he almost smothered me with the bag." PJ touched her throat and closed her eyes.

Anger burned in Chuck. This was the second time PJ had almost been killed and he hadn't been there to stop it. "The bastard."

A tear slipped from the corner of her eye and trailed across her cheekbone into her hair as she lay on the ground. "All I could think of was you and Charlie."

Chuck could barely contain the anger he felt at whoever was doing this to PJ. He couldn't lash out, not knowing who it was and with PJ lying in front of him so helpless. He had to take care of her first.

"After he stuck the stick in my mouth, I must have passed out." PJ sat up, swayed and would have lay back except that Chuck slipped an arm around her shoulders.

"What do you mean, stuck a stick in your mouth?" Chuck asked.

"I don't know. I was half out of it, too busy breathing air after almost suffocating. He held my head back and jaw down and scraped something around the inside of my mouth." She pressed a hand to her cheek. "At least I think. It's all a bit fuzzy." She stared up at him. "I'm so glad you found me. Much longer, and I'd have had a helluva sunburn." She laughed shakily.

Chuck pulled her against his chest and held her tight.

"Easy. I'm feeling a little guarded about my breathing." She laid a hand on his chest.

Chuck swallowed hard to chase back the lump in his throat. She could have died, and he had been so close and known nothing about it.

"PJ? Chuck?" Cara Jo's voice called out from the door of the diner.

"We're behind the Dumpster," Chuck called out. He scooped PJ up from the ground and stood, ignoring the pain in his leg.

"I can walk." PJ slipped an arm around his shoulder. "But this is nice."

"Let's get you hydrated." He stepped out from behind the trash container, forcing himself not to limp.

Cara Jo and Mrs. K rushed forward.

"Oh, my God." Cara Jo, her eyes wide, touched PJ's arm. She carried Charlie on her hip. "Are you all right?"

"I'm fine. Chuck's just playing the he-man." She frowned up at him. "Really, I can walk."

"Let him carry you," Mrs. K said. "If you age like I did, someday you'll wish he still could." She patted PJ's hand, her eyes tearing. "Honey, I'm so sorry. I should have taken that darned trash out."

"Mrs. K, I'm fine. I wasn't going to let you do my job for me. Besides, you couldn't have known. And what if he'd attacked you?"

"He wasn't after Mrs. K." Chuck's arms tightened around her. "Whoever did this was waiting for you. He knew you took the trash out at two and that you'd be alone." Chuck knew this without a doubt. "And I know what he was after."

"DNA?" PJ asked.

PJ SAT ON a gurney in one of the examination rooms in the emergency room of Wild Oak Canyon Hospital, swinging her leg, ready to get the heck out of there. "Why are we still here? The doctor told me I'm fine—no lasting damage, and the bruises will heal in a couple weeks."

"Hank's on his way. He wanted you to stay put until he got here."

PJ's eyes narrowed. "Why?"

Chuck didn't want to get into an argument. Not now. Not when he'd almost lost her. "You can guess why."

"He wants to do that DNA sample thing?" PJ shook her head. "Why the heck didn't you say so in the first place?"

"You'll do it?"

PJ nodded. "After what happened a little while ago, I'm feeling the need to know what everyone else is eager to attack me to find out. If it will help us catch the jerk terrorizing us, I'm all for it."

Chuck smiled at her and caressed her cheek. "That's my girl."

"In the meantime, do you think Cara Jo's okay with Charlie?"

"She and Mrs. K are out in the waiting room providing her entertainment."

PJ frowned. "You don't think Charlie will catch anything here, do you?"

"Hopefully not. I don't want her too far out of our sight. I think she'll be safe here in the hospital until we can take her back to Hank's."

A nurse entered the examination room carrying two packages and two vials. "You have a visitor."

Hank Derringer followed her in.

"Normally, I don't let anyone back here but family." The nurse smiled. "Mr. Derringer says he might be just that." She ripped open one of the packages containing a stick with a swab at the end. "Ms. Franks, just to be certain, do you agree to this DNA paternity test?"

PJ drew in a long breath. "For my entire life, I'd believed my father was dead." She laughed, a short, not very amused sound. "And this test might prove that he isn't, and that my mother lied to me."

"To protect you, dear," Hank interjected. He reached out and patted her hand. "Whether or not we are blood related, I'll always consider you family."

She looked up into Hank's kind face. This was the type of man she'd always pictured her father would look like. A man she wished he'd been. "I always thought family never lied to each other."

"I'm sorry, my dear. Had I known Alana was pregnant when I sent her away…"

PJ raised her hand. "It doesn't matter now. I remember my mother saying, *'Don't borrow trouble, Peggy.'*" PJ's lips twisted. "For all we know you aren't my father. And I still won't know who he is."

"PJ, we need to narrow it down. Whoever stole your sample earlier today will know something soon. We need to know what we're up against." Chuck took her hand and squeezed it. "But it's totally up to you. It's your choice, and I'll stand behind whatever you decide."

PJ's glance shifted to Hank. "And you, Mr. Derringer? If I decide not to do this, will you respect my wishes?"

"My dear PJ, you make the decision. I'll stand behind you either way. You and Charlie mean more to me than a test result."

PJ turned to the nurse. "Let's do this." She opened her mouth.

The nurse swabbed the inside of her cheek and stuck the swab into a tube. She performed the same procedure on Hank. Then she put both vials into a padded envelope and sealed it. "Do you want to do the honors of placing this in the mail?"

"Yes." PJ took the package from her. "Can we leave now? I want to see Charlie."

"Yes, my dear." Hank helped her off the gurney. "She was giggling with Cara Jo and Mrs. Kinsley in the lobby when I came through."

"Good. She's happy. And if we hurry, we can get to the post office before it closes." Now that she had the samples, she was more eager to get the results than she wanted to admit to Hank or Chuck.

"PJ, you have the choice of what lab to send the DNA samples to." Hank followed her out of the room. "And they will do a fine job, no doubt. But I'd feel a lot better if the samples were hand-delivered to a lab in San Antonio that performs these kinds of tests by the hundreds. I could have it hand-delivered and put an expedite on it, and we could get the results back in two days."

PJ stopped and faced Hank. "And how long will it take if I send it to the lab indicated on the package?"

"It can take anywhere between five days and a week, depending on how soon the samples are delivered and how big a backlog the lab has." Hank's lips pressed together. "If we send it to San Antonio, it requires that you trust me to handle it."

She raised her brows. "No more lies?"

Hank nodded. "My dear, I've never lied to you."

Her eyes narrowed. "No more lying by omission?"

"Agreed."

She handed him the package. "I trust you, Hank."

Hank hugged her. "Thank you for that." Then he chucked Charlie beneath the chin and left them standing in the lobby to hurry out to the parking lot.

PJ took Charlie from Cara Jo and hugged her close. "It's been a crazy day, hasn't it, sweetie?"

"Glad you came out when you did." Cara Jo

shifted the diaper bag to her shoulder. "Charlie's getting hungry, and there wasn't a bottle in the bag."

Chuck pressed a hand to PJ's back and guided her toward the exit. "Let's get you out to the truck."

Charlie leaned into PJ's neck, found her fist and made loud sucking noises.

PJ laughed. "Yeah, Charlie, I know it's time for supper."

Cara Jo and Mrs. Kinsley drove off in Cara Jo's car.

Chuck helped PJ into the truck and handed Charlie into her lap. "Want me to wait outside?" he asked.

PJ shrugged, pulling her blouse out of her waistband. "It's up to you. I'm perfectly comfortable nursing her in front of you. Question is, are you comfortable around a woman nursing?"

"I'm fine. Let me get the AC going for you and Charlie." Chuck rounded to the driver's side and slid in. He inserted the key and cranked the engine, setting the AC on cool. With dusk settling in on the little town, the temperature had begun to drop, but not enough to keep them from sweating in the closed confines of the cab.

Despite his best efforts to keep his eyes averted to give PJ some privacy, Chuck's gaze strayed more than once to the baby suckling at her mother's breast. Each time a sense of warmth spread through him, filling him with a sense of something he couldn't quite put his finger on.

All he knew was this felt right. Being with PJ and Charlie. PJ trusting him enough to nurse their baby in front of him, and no words needed to fill a comfortable silence.

"She's so tired, she's falling asleep." PJ shifted Charlie and dropped her shirt over her bare breast. "We can go home now."

"Don't you mean back to Hank's?"

"No. I want to be at my own place with my own stuff."

"I don't know. With all that's been happening, I don't feel like I can keep you safe enough."

PJ reached out and touched his arm. "You're doing a pretty darned good job so far. I trust that you'll continue."

He nodded and climbed down from his seat, rounding to her side of the truck. PJ handed a sleeping Charlie to him, and he carefully buckled her into her car seat in the back, pressing a kiss to her milky cheek.

Charlie smelled of baby powder and soft-scented shampoo. He could get used to having that smell around. He tucked a light blanket around her and closed the door.

As he got back into the truck, he glanced toward PJ.

She stared out the window, a frown on her face.

"What's wrong?" he asked.

"That SUV." She pointed. "It's been sitting there for a long time."

"Might be someone visiting a relative in the hospital."

"No. It's not empty. Every once in a while, I see the silhouette of someone's head through the tinted glass." PJ shrugged and sat back against the seat. "I'm getting paranoid."

"You have a right to be." Chuck shifted into Drive and eased toward the SUV. "Wouldn't hurt to run the license plate. Got a pen?"

"Hold on." PJ dived for her purse, rummaging through until she pulled an old receipt and a pen from the depths. "Got it."

Before Chuck could move toward the SUV, the vehicle pulled out of the parking lot and turned right.

"Did you catch the license plate?"

"No, it was too far away and obscured by a frame around it."

"I'm going to follow." Chuck punched the accelerator with his foot and tore across the parking lot to the street.

PJ touched his arm. "No, Chuck, not this time. We have Charlie with us. I don't want her in the line of fire. Not that I think they'll shoot at us."

"But why take the chance?" Chuck hesitated before pulling out onto the street in the opposite direction the SUV had taken. "I'll call the police and have them keep a look out for it."

"I like that idea better." PJ glanced over her shoulder at Charlie. "I need to get Charlie home. She needs a bath, and I need something to eat." As if to emphasize her words, her stomach growled.

Chuck grinned. "How about we eat at the diner tonight?"

"I'd love that. I'm too tired to think about fixing a meal."

"Then it's a date. You, me and Charlie."

PJ settled back in her seat, a slight smile tugging at her lips. She could get used to having Chuck around. He made her feel safe. Not for the first time, she questioned her decision to push him away a year ago. The only conclusion she'd come to was that she'd been afraid. Afraid to love him too much and lose him, like every other important person in her life.

PJ's gaze shifted to the baby sleeping in the backseat. She loved Charlie more than she loved her own life. If anything were to happen to her baby daughter, she didn't know how she'd cope. But as Chuck said, there were no guarantees.

Would PJ give up the time she had with Charlie now, banking on the possibility of losing her in the future?

No.

So what was the difference?

She glanced at Chuck from beneath her lashes. He'd aged in the year he'd been gone. The lines around his eyes were more pronounced, and the shadows beneath them spoke of the sorrow and tragedy of the war he'd fought.

PJ wanted to hold him and wipe away the terrible images he must have stored in his memories. He'd been angry with her for keeping news of his daughter's birth from him. Would he ever forgive her for that? Would he ever learn to trust her again?

The drive ended at the back of the resort.

PJ jumped down from her seat before Chuck could get around to her side and hold her door. She didn't want him to do nice things for her. Not when she was so confused by the blossoming feelings she harbored and the wrongs that stood between them.

Chuck unbuckled Charlie and lifted her, seat and all, carrying her as if she weighed less than a kitten.

Thankful for Chuck to help out, PJ followed him up the steps. "I'd like to shower and change before dinner. I still feel like I have gravel and dirt in my hair and skin."

"Take your time. I'll keep an eye on Charlie. And leave the apartment door open so that I can keep an eye on the hallway, as well."

PJ grabbed her bathrobe, brush and soaps and hurried toward the bathroom, leaving the door to the apartment open.

At her last glance, Chuck had scooted the recliner to a position from which he could see the outer hallway and the baby crib. He stood with Charlie in his arms. "Go on, we'll be okay."

She hesitated, taking in the picture of the big cowboy holding the tiny baby in the crook of his arm.

Chuck winked.

PJ scooted into the bathroom, her face and body burning with something far different from embarrassment. A chilly shower did nothing to cool the fire building at her core. After scrubbing the dirt and grime off her body, she hopped out of the bathtub and ran a towel across her sensitized skin, imagining a pair of work-roughened hands skimming over her instead.

Still burning, with no relief in sight, PJ pulled jeans over her hips, snapped a bra in place and dragged a T-shirt over her head. A quick brush through her hair, and she stood with her hand hovering over the doorknob, her breathing faster than usual and her heart thumping against her ribs.

Maybe Charlie will sleep a little longer while Chuck and I...

PJ sucked in a deep breath and stepped out into the hall, fully expecting to see Chuck sitting in the chair, Charlie in his arms.

The chair was empty.

PJ frowned and hurried toward the apartment,

every bad scenario her fevered mind could think of running through her head.

"Chuck?" she said as she stepped into the apartment.

"Hey, where's the fire?" He snagged her arm and pulled her into his embrace. "Did you miss me?" He pushed the door closed behind her.

"Don't scare me like that."

"I was just straightening the picture on the wall. It's okay."

"I didn't see you and Charlie." She closed her eyes and let go of a long, steadying breath. "This situation is making me crazy."

"Not nearly as crazy as it's making me." He pushed a damp strand of hair behind her ear. "Being this close to you…" Chuck bent, his lips claiming hers.

The kiss started out soft, gentle, almost a brush of two mouths.

PJ's hands slid around Chuck's neck and she deepened the contact, dragging him closer, her hips pressing against his. Her tongue pushed past his teeth and stroked his in long, sensual thrusts. All the pent-up emotions of the past couple of days erupted inside, and she couldn't hold back.

Chuck backed her against the wall and lifted her, wrapping her legs around his waist, never taking his mouth from hers.

The heat intensified, the need to be naked flaming the inferno until the sound of a baby crying pulled PJ back to earth.

Chuck let her legs drop to the floor. "We need to talk."

"Yes, we do." PJ disengaged her arms from around his neck and stepped around him, pressing her hands to her burning cheeks. "Later. Charlie needs me."

A diaper change and a few minutes of nursing later, the fires had cooled but weren't forgotten. PJ carried Charlie out to the living room, ready to have that conversation.

Chuck had his back to her, his cell phone to his ear. "We figured as much. It has to be someone nearby. Can he narrow it down to an address?"

PJ frowned and circled around Chuck, studying his face as he spoke on the phone.

"We will. No, we'll be staying in town tonight. Thanks, Hank."

Chuck clicked the off button and met PJ's eyes. "Brandon, the computer guru, has the IP address of the hacker."

Chapter Thirteen

Chuck wished he hadn't told PJ about the IP address as soon as the words were out of his mouth.

"Where is it?" PJ grabbed the diaper bag and crammed diapers into it, and then she snatched a bottle of breast milk out of the freezer and stuffed it into the side pocket. "What are you waiting for? Let's get there. I have a few choice words for the guy who has been making my life miserable."

Chuck shook his head. "We can't go."

PJ stood at the door to the apartment, diaper bag slung over one shoulder, Charlie on her opposite hip. "Why?"

"I want to nail the guy as badly as you do, but Brandon only has the IP address. He's still tracing it to a physical address."

The light in PJ's eyes faded, and her shoulders sagged. "Well, darn. And here I was getting all hopeful."

"Come on, we'll get that dinner I promised and maybe by the time we've eaten, Brandon will have performed his miracle and found the address."

Chuck led the way down the steps, careful to scan the parking lot in the dull light emitted from the one security light. As he stepped away from the building, the motion-sensing lights blinked on, illuminating the corners halfway down the building, making it a lot easier to see someone who might be coming to attack them.

Throughout dinner, Chuck and PJ sat in strained silence, both listening for Chuck's cell phone to ring. It didn't happen. By the time they'd eaten, Charlie had fallen asleep, and PJ yawned so wide Chuck was afraid she might break her jaw.

"We might as well call it a night," Chuck finally announced. He'd wanted to hear from Brandon as badly as PJ had. "Brandon will call when he has it."

"What's taking him so long?" PJ stifled yet another yawn.

"These things take time." Chuck gathered the infant carrier with Charlie in it and carried her up the stairs to the apartment. Once inside, he laid her in her crib.

PJ stripped the baby's clothes, changed her diaper and slipped her pajamas on.

Charlie stirred but didn't awaken. Apparently the excitement of being at the hospital and then the diner had taken its toll on the baby. She was out for the night.

Which left Chuck relatively alone with PJ.

"If you think you and Charlie will be all right, I'll hit the shower."

"Are you staying here or in your apartment?"

He couldn't tell if she wanted him there or if she was trying to get rid of him, but he wasn't going to give her a choice. Not after all that had happened. "I'm staying here."

She nodded, her gaze sliding away from his. "Good. I'll get you a blanket and pillow."

Chuck suppressed a groan. Another night on the couch or in the lounge chair so close to where PJ would be sleeping. He should have expected that, but deep down, he'd hoped their previous night's sleeping arrangements had meant something more than a blanket and pillow on the couch tonight.

Just as well. Without the protection of Hank's security system and additional firepower, Chuck was on his own to protect PJ and Charlie. He'd have to focus his thoughts out of the bedroom in order to keep them safe.

He hurried through a lukewarm shower, frustrated that he couldn't make the water any colder or that he had to get out so soon. The longer he stayed away from his girls, the more likely someone else could get to them.

Several times he'd shut off the shower to listen for footsteps on the landing. Each time, he shook his head, thinking he'd grown more paranoid than ever.

After barely five minutes, he jammed his feet into clean jeans and padded barefoot back to the apartment, carrying his shirt. He entered using a key PJ had loaned him, careful not to wake the baby, and then he closed the door behind him and locked the dead bolt.

PJ stood in the bedroom, pulling her T-shirt over her head.

Chuck stood transfixed, unable to look away.

When she'd tossed the shirt aside, she glanced up, her gaze capturing his. A soft pink blush rose up her neck, filling her cheeks, and her mouth rounded into a pretty O shape.

She didn't try to cover herself, nor did she flash an angry look his way. Instead, PJ reached behind her and flicked the catch on her bra, releasing it. The straps loosened, and she let them slide down her arms to drop to the floor.

"Peggy Jane," Chuck moaned. "You sure you want to do that?"

She braced one hand on her jeans-clad hip and raised her brows. "Would I be standing here half-naked if I wasn't sure?" she challenged. A quick glance at the crib and she strode out of the bedroom into the living room, stopping directly in front of him. "Are you going to stand there and stare, or do something?"

He chuckled. "What did you have in mind?"

"This." She lifted his hand and placed it on her breast. "And this." PJ plucked the T-shirt he'd been holding out of his hand and tossed it onto the couch, and then she guided his fingers to her face, pressing her cheek into his palm. "Do I have to do it all?"

"So far, I have no complaints. Except one..." He

tipped her head back. "We're both overdressed." Past the point of teasing, Chuck pulled her into his arms and crushed her lips with his.

PJ worked the button loose on his jeans, slid the zipper down and shoved his pants over his hips.

Chuck did the same, going a step further by sliding the denim down her long, slender legs until she stepped free. God, she had great legs, and when they wrapped around him…

He lifted her off her feet.

PJ locked her ankles behind him, pressing her warm wetness down over his straining member.

He thrust up into her, her tight channel taking his full length, encasing him in delicious heat.

PJ's head dropped back, her hair falling down to brush against his knuckles.

He lifted her and thrust into her again.

She moaned. "Faster."

He backed her against the wall, held her hips and pounded into her again and again until she writhed, her fingers gripping his arms.

The tension built, the fierce longing he'd carried for this woman for such a long time exploding in his veins, sending him catapulting over the edge of reason.

As he neared the peak, PJ's heels dug into his buttocks, her fingernails clawed his shoulders and her body grew rigid.

One final thrust, and his insides detonated in a

burst of sensations so powerful he thought he might have died.

He held her hips, reveling in the wonder that was their most intimate connection.

When he finally came back to himself, he buried his face in her neck.

Her fingers combed through his hair. "Chuck?"

"Hmm?"

"My legs are cramping."

Chuck carried her to the bedroom and laid her on the bed. Then he crawled in beside her and spooned her body against his, burying his face in the side of her neck. The herbal scent of her hair surrounded him, reminding him of the days before he'd deployed, when they'd been carefree and in love.

"Remember that night at the swimming hole in Willow Creek?"

"Uh-huh." He nuzzled her throat, pressing kisses against her soft skin. "You almost stepped on a snake."

She batted at his hands. "Is that all you remember?"

"No. I remember it was the first time we'd made love."

"I was afraid you didn't really like me."

"I was afraid I liked you too much, and would scare you away." And he had. "Do you ever wish we could go back?"

"No," PJ stated with a certain conviction in the one-syllable word. "I wouldn't change anything, because if I did, we wouldn't have Charlie. And I can't imagine life without my sweet baby."

"Agreed." Chuck stroked the length of her arm and down across the curve of her hip. She felt like heaven to him.

"What are we going to do about us?" PJ whispered.

"I suggest we take it one day at a time."

"What if we don't have another day? What if this maniac gets to me when you're not there? What will happen to Charlie?"

"I'm not going to let anything happen to either one of you."

She rolled over and stared up into his eyes. "Promise?"

He cupped her cheek, and with his lips hovering over hers, he said, "I'll do my best." And prayed his best was good enough. A little Afghan boy had died because Chuck hadn't been able to protect him from his own village. What made him think he could protect PJ and Charlie from a man they couldn't seem to locate?

PJ drifted to sleep, her body warm and soft against Chuck.

He lay for a long time, fighting a rising sense of panic, telling himself that losing focus now would do neither one of them any good. Afraid to go to sleep, he lay awake, remembering all the good times he and PJ had before he deployed, hoping that when he went to sleep, he wouldn't go back to that place that haunted him since he'd stormed into a Taliban stronghold and wrought his revenge on the killers of children.

He must have drifted to sleep sometime during the night despite all his efforts not to. The next conscious thought was of a buzzing vibration sound on the nightstand beside him.

When he opened his eyes, he noted the gray, predawn light filtering through the edges of the blinds, and the irritating, vibrating buzzing started again.

Chuck reached for the telephone before it rattled against the wood of the nightstand again. He hit the talk button but didn't say anything until he'd rolled out of bed and strode into the living room. "Bolton here," he said softly.

"Chuck, we have an address." Hank's voice cleared the remaining haze of sleep from Chuck's brain.

"Where is it?"

Hank gave him the details. "I'm going to call the police with it, as well."

"Give me a few minutes before you do. I want to be there when they arrest the guy."

"I'm on my way in from the ranch. I want to be there, as well."

Chuck clicked the phone off, grabbed his clothes from the floor where he'd left them the night before and dressed. When he sat to pull his boots on, a noise made him turn.

PJ stood with a sheet wrapped around her naked

body, her hair tousled and her face still flushed from sleep. "Are you leaving?"

"Hank called."

She blinked and took another step into the room. "They have the address?"

He nodded.

"I'm coming with you." She turned toward the bedroom.

Chuck pulled his second boot on, stood and crossed the room. He rubbed his hands down her arms. "The police will be handling the arrest, and we don't know if it'll be dangerous. I'd rather you and Charlie stayed away from it all."

PJ's gaze shifted to the crib, where Charlie was just beginning to stir. "I guess we wouldn't have time to get ready, anyway." She glanced up at him, her brows lowered. "You'll be careful?"

He brushed his lips across hers. "You bet."

Gripping the sheet with one hand, PJ raised the other and pulled him back, deepening the kiss. "Come by the diner when it's over. I want a full report."

"Yes, ma'am." He swatted her bottom and headed out the door. "Lock it behind me." He left, praying this would be the arrest to end the troubles. Then he and PJ could sort things out.

PJ SHOT THE bolt on the door, returned to the bedroom, fed Charlie and dressed for work. Still not feeling comfortable about leaving Charlie at the day care, PJ called Dana, hoping she was off that day since she worked at the day care only three days a week.

"As a matter of fact, today is my day off," Dana said.

"Do you already have plans? I'll understand if you do."

"Relax, PJ. I'd be happy to stay with Charlie while you work. Then maybe you can fill me in on all that's been happening with you. I can't believe someone actually bugged the day care."

"Honey, that's not all."

"Hold that thought," Dana said. "I can be there in ten minutes."

PJ hung up and made a mad dash through the apartment, picking up the discarded clothing from her crazy hot sex with Chuck in the living room. Her cheeks burned at the image etched permanently in her mind of making love with Chuck against the wall.

She'd never look at that wall the same. PJ's pulse pounded with the same intensity of the night before. Forcing herself to look away, she hurried to the bedroom to make the bed, smoothing the sheets that still smelled of Chuck.

A knock on the door startled her back to reality and set her pulse racing.

"PJ, it's me, Dana." Her friend's voice came through the door.

PJ took several deep, steadying breaths and

forced herself to look normal when she opened the door for Dana.

Dana stepped in, her gaze on PJ's face, her eyes narrowing. "Wow, PJ, you look different."

PJ pressed a hand to her cheeks as they burned hotter.

Her friend's eyes widened, and a grin spread across her face. "You did it with Chuck, didn't you?"

"I d-don't know what you're talking about," PJ stammered.

"I knew it! You and Chuck are back together, aren't you?" She grabbed PJ's hand. "That has to be the reason for the glow."

"I'm glowing?" PJ laughed. "Now you're just being silly."

"No, my dear, you are most certainly glowing." Still holding PJ's hand, she marched her into the bedroom and made her stand in front of the mirror over the dresser. "See?"

PJ stared at the stranger in the mirror. Her cheeks were flushed, and her eyes sparkled.

Dana grinned beside her. "That's love, sweetie."

PJ's heart stopped and then skipped into gear again, pounding against her ribs.

"I take it you two have figured everything out," Dana was saying. "It's about time."

PJ shook her head. "No, no, we haven't." Her brows dipped, and the flush paled in her cheeks. She turned away from the mirror and stared at the floor. "We keep saying we have to talk, but we end up making love instead."

Dana gripped her arms and forced her to look at her. "Hey, that's a good start."

"But nothing's resolved." PJ stared into her friend's eyes, tears welling in her own. She pulled away and walked across the room. "I don't know where this is going or if he'll stick around once they arrest the man harassing me."

"They found him? Oh, thank God." Dana lifted Charlie from her crib and held her in her arms.

"If all goes well…" PJ stopped at the window, staring out into the parking lot. "They'll be arresting someone any minute now."

"You hear that, Charlie?" Dana kissed the baby's cheek. "We're going to have a great day."

"I have to go to work."

Dana leaned over and kissed PJ's cheek. "You and Chuck were meant for each other. It'll work out, just you wait and see."

PJ ducked her face and swung away, afraid Dana might see the sudden rush of tears in her eyes. "Thanks for coming on such short notice, Dana. We'll talk later."

"We'll be here, waiting for Mommy and Daddy to come home." Dana held up one of Charlie's hands and waved. "Bye-bye, Mommy."

PJ waved at the two and then left the apartment, locking the door behind her and running down the stairs and around the building to the diner.

If the police arrested the man responsible for the attacks, then for all intents and purposes, Chuck would be done with his assignment to protect her and Charlie. Hank would send him on another job, possibly more dangerous than this one had turned out.

Where would that leave her and Charlie?

For the next hour, PJ could barely focus on waiting tables. Every time someone stepped in the door, she spun to see if it was Chuck.

The kind, older Hispanic gentleman, Señor Iglesias, caught her arm as she tried to pour ice water into his coffee mug. "Señorita Franks, that is not necessary."

"I'm so sorry. Let me get you a fresh cup."

"No need. I sense you are disturbed. Is there anything I can do to help?"

"No, I'm just a bit distracted. I'm sorry I ruined your coffee."

"You are much too pretty to be so worried."

"It's just that…" She shook her head. "Never mind."

"I am your only customer at this moment, so *por favor,* sit. Maybe talking will help."

PJ sank into the seat across from the man. His kind eyes and the sincere look on his face made her want to spill her guts to this stranger. "So much has happened in the past few days."

"I heard there have been some attacks on you as

well as another young man." Señor Iglesias frowned. "Have the police found the person responsible?"

"I hope so. I would hate for anything to happen to my little girl."

"Ah, a sweet *bambina*." Señor Iglesias smiled. "Does she look like her beautiful mother?"

"No, she's more like her father than me. She's everything to me. If anything were to happen to Charlie...I couldn't live without her."

"I know what you mean. A mother's love for her child is strong. A father's love isn't always as deep as it should be. His expectations can be too high, and he can be too stubborn to see. Mother and child have a special bond."

"You have children, don't you, Señor Iglesias? You must know how heartbroken a parent would feel to lose one."

His dark eyes clouded. "I have lost a child."

When PJ's brows furrowed, the older man raised a hand. "Not to death, but to a life I could not approve of. He turned his back on his *familia*. I truly believe his mother died of a broken heart."

"I'm sorry." PJ reached across the table and touched the old man's arm. "She must have loved him dearly."

"*Sí.*" Señor Iglesias covered her hand with his. "You remind me of her."

"Thank you."

"If ever you need anything, *por favor,* call on me.

I will help you in any way possible." He handed her a business card. "My apologies, *está en Español*."

"Numbers are easily translated. Thank you." PJ patted the man's arm and tucked the card into her apron pocket. "Now I'd better get back to work so that I can pay rent." She smiled and pushed to her feet. "Enjoy the rest of your stay in Wild Oak Canyon. Despite the trouble lately, it's a wonderful place to live."

He nodded. "Thank you for entertaining an old man."

PJ slipped out of the diner and back up to her apartment, anxious to see Charlie.

The lock clicked, and she pushed the door open.

"Oh, PJ." Dana stared across at her. "I'm so glad you're here."

"Where's Charlie?"

Dana smiled. "Relax. She's in her crib, and she's hungry."

PJ sucked in air and let it out. Thank God, Charlie was all right.

IT TOOK FORTY-FIVE minutes for the sheriff to arrange for assistance from the Texas state troopers and get them in place before making a move on the street location of the IP address. Chuck stood by with Hank outside the perimeter of the police-barricaded streets. Chuck wanted to be in on the action, to come face-to-face with PJ's attacker.

Hank touched his arm. "I know you want to be in there."

"I'm not good at waiting." It was the primary reason he'd been booted from the army. He'd disobeyed orders and gone off in a fit of rage to find and kill the people responsible for torturing a small boy, and he'd gotten himself shot in the process.

"They'll let us know soon enough."

"Not soon enough for me." Chuck paced back and forth beside a sheriff's cruiser, parked sideways across the road.

The neighborhood was barely awake, and most people had yet to leave for work. One by one, lights blinked on inside the homes as alarms woke residents.

Hank's eyes narrowed as he stared at the house the state police were targeting. "Looks like they're moving in."

Chuck stopped pacing and squinted into the eastern sunrise. "Finally."

The house was surrounded by armed men. The Wild Oak Canyon temporary sheriff, Deputy Johnny Owen, stepped up to the door, weapon drawn and pounded. "This is the sheriff's department. Open up."

Several long seconds passed before the door opened and a man wearing a bathrobe peered out, blinking sleepily. He spoke to the deputy, his eyes wide, hands raised.

"I can't hear what he's saying." Chuck leaned forward, as if that would help.

"Me, either."

The man in the bathrobe was led outside by a deputy. A woman, also wearing a robe, stepped outside carrying a little boy.

"The deputy's going in," Hank said.

The deputy and several other uniformed men entered the house. After a few minutes they emerged and spoke with the homeowner again.

The man pointed to the house next door. A For Sale sign leaned crookedly in the overgrown yard. The blinds in the windows were closed, and the house appeared vacant.

"What do you suppose is going on?" Hank asked.

"I don't know." Chuck could barely stand still. He wanted to be close enough to hear what the man in the bathrobe was saying.

The deputy and two more uniforms crossed to the empty house and tried the knob on the front door. When it didn't open, they rounded the side to the back.

Several minutes later, they emerged from the front door.

Deputy Owen pointed to the houses surrounding the empty one and the deputies took off, knocking on those doors, waking residents. Dogs barked and children peeked around parents' legs.

"They're canvassing the neighborhood," Hank said.

"Why aren't they arresting the man in the bathrobe?" Chuck's fists clenched and unclenched.

"Maybe he's not the person they're after."

"Holy hell." Chuck jammed his hands into his pockets. "This can't be a dead end."

Deputy Owen broke away from the man in the bathrobe and strode toward Hank.

Hank straightened. "What's going on?"

"The address you gave us is the right one."

"Then why no arrest?" Chuck demanded.

The deputy frowned at Chuck and then addressed Hank. "He has a Wi-Fi network set up without a password. Apparently someone tapped into it. I suspect it was the person using the vacant house next door. We found candy wrappers and soda bottles inside. My team is collecting evidence and fingerprints now, and we're asking neighbors if they've seen anyone going into or around the house in the past few days."

Chuck closed his eyes. "What you're saying is, you still have no idea who's tapping into Mr. Derringer's computers or who attacked PJ and Danny?"

Deputy Owen shrugged. "We don't even know for certain the events are connected."

"They are," Hank said.

"We'll let you know if we learn anything from the neighbors. Other than that, we can't arrest a man for having an unsecured router." The deputy shook his head. "In the meantime, we try to fit the pieces together."

"Damn." Chuck turned away from the scene.

Hank rested a hand on his shoulder. "The police will find out who was in the house."

"When? Today? Tomorrow? After something happens to PJ?"

"We're doing the best with the resources we have."

"Excuse me." A woman walked up to Deputy Owen.

"Yes, ma'am." The deputy faced the woman.

"A deputy asked my husband if he'd seen any-one coming through here in the past few days. He hadn't, but I remember seeing someone. I'm not sure it means anything, but you never know."

"Who?" Chuck asked before the deputy could.

The woman's gaze shifted from Chuck back to Deputy Owen. "Mr. Bergman's grandson walks through here every day going to and from work at the hardware store. I'm sure it's nothing, but I thought you'd like to know." She wrung her hands. "Are you looking for someone dangerous? Should we, as residents, be scared?"

The deputy frowned. "We're not sure. Lock your doors at night, and you should be all right."

"I told my husband we should lock our doors." The woman walked away, shaking her head and muttering about her spouse.

"I'll send someone over to the hardware store. Mr. Bergman opens pretty early."

"Mind if we come along?"

"No." The deputy held up a finger. "As long as you let me do all the talking."

"Absolutely," Hank agreed.

Chuck clamped his lips shut and nodded.

Rather than walking the two blocks to the hardware store, Hank and Chuck drove over in Chuck's pickup.

The acting sheriff and a couple of his deputies had pulled into the space in front of the store. Hank and Chuck entered behind them.

Mr. Bergman was wiping his hands on a rag. "Good morning, deputies, Mr. Johnson, Hank. What brings you here so early?"

"We'd like to speak to your grandson, Ross Felton," the deputy said.

The store owner frowned. "Ross doesn't usually come in until around ten."

"Do you know where we can find him?"

"He lives in the apartment above Mrs. Grissom's garage on Fifth Street. Why? What's he done?"

"We don't know. We just want to ask him some questions." The deputy nodded toward Mr. Bergman. "Is your grandson familiar with computers?"

Bergman snorted. "That's all the boy did when he lived with his mother. He played games and sat behind his computer rather than get outside and do a decent day's work."

"Has he said anything to you about Hank Derringer or PJ Franks?"

Mr. Bergman's glance strayed to Hank. "Not that I've heard. Isn't Miss Franks the waitress at the diner?"

"Yes," Hank answered.

"Other than waiting on his table, I can't imagine he even knows who she is. He doesn't socialize much." Mr. Bergman shook his head. "He doesn't do much of anything, from what I can see. I can barely get him to show up for work."

"Thank you, Mr. Bergman." Deputy Owen led the other deputies out to the sidewalk.

Hank hurried after the deputy, questioning him as they walked.

Mr. Bergman caught Chuck's arm as he turned to follow Hank out the door. "Is Ross in trouble?"

"I really can't say."

"He's always been a challenge to his mother, and he's been a pain in the butt working here, but I like to think he's got a heart in there somewhere behind all that attitude."

"I'm sure he does."

"His mother has gone through a lot already. Ross's father was abusive. He used to hit my daughter and the boy when they lived with him. Whatever happens, please give him the benefit of the doubt. If not for Ross, then for his mother." Mr. Bergman let go of Chuck's arm.

Chuck nodded and left the store. His desire to choke the life out of the man responsible for attacking PJ warred with the old man's desire to give his grandson a break to spare his daughter.

Why did the world have to be so messed up? Abusive fathers, delinquent sons, computer hackers and

Taliban retribution. It all made Chuck's own falling-out with his father seem insignificant.

Hank met him on the sidewalk. "The sheriff is on his way to Felton's apartment. In the meantime, we have bigger trouble coming."

"What do you mean?"

Hank held out his cell phone with a photo on it.

It was a picture of PJ in her waitress uniform. Beneath it was a text message.

Chuck grabbed the phone and read: If you don't want the Mexican drug lords to know who the waitress really is, bring one million dollars to the abandoned Ferguson barn tonight at midnight. Alone. Don't be late. You don't have much time.

Chapter Fourteen

PJ checked on Charlie several times during the day, and everything seemed all right. After a slow morning at the diner, Cara Jo told her to take off before lunch and get some rest.

Chuck and Hank had yet to call with an update on the arrest, and the waiting was killing PJ.

She stopped by her apartment prior to heading for the sheriff's office.

"Heard anything?" Dana asked as PJ stepped through the door.

PJ sighed, dumping her purse on the counter. "Nothing."

"I would have thought Chuck and Hank would have stopped at the diner by now."

"All I can think is that the arrest didn't go as planned."

"Are you going to wait here for news? Charlie will be happy, won't you, baby?" Dana tickled Charlie's belly.

The baby giggled and batted her hands at Dana's face.

PJ lifted her daughter into her arms and kissed her soft cheek. "I'm behind on a couple of assignments for school. If you don't mind staying a few more hours, I'm going to run by the sheriff's department and then the library. I'll be home before five." She hugged Charlie and kissed her again before handing her back to Dana.

"Take your time." Dana perched Charlie on her hip and smiled at PJ. "Charlie and I have been having a great time, and I'm catching up on my television programs." Dana waved her toward the door. "Go on. I've got you on speed dial, and I'll keep the doors locked."

"Thanks, Dana. I won't be any longer than I have to."

"Be careful out there."

"Will do."

PJ peered through the peephole before opening the apartment door. When she closed it behind her, she waited to hear the click of the dead bolt Chuck had installed before she headed to the parking lot and her car.

As she scanned the area all around her, she was hyperaware of her surroundings, determined not to be a victim again. Before she climbed into her car, she checked the backseat in case someone was hiding on the floor, waiting for his chance to nab her.

PJ laughed shakily as she climbed into her car, locked the doors and took off across town to the sheriff's office. When she arrived she parked in front, next to a cruiser.

Deputy Owen stepped out of the building at the same time PJ got out of her car.

She hurried forward. "Sir, can you tell me how the arrest went this morning?"

Deputy Owen frowned. "It didn't." He moved to go around her.

PJ's heart plummeted, and she refused to be side-stepped until she got answers. "What do you mean, it didn't?"

"The computer at the address had an unsecured router with Wi-Fi capability."

"I'm sorry, I don't understand."

"Anyone could have used the man's IP address to hack into Mr. Derringer's system and send you the messages you've received."

"Oh." PJ stood still as Deputy Owen went around her to his vehicle. So much for feeling safer in Wild Oak Canyon. Basically, they were right back at square one. Then why the heck hadn't she heard anything from Chuck or Hank?

PJ climbed back into her car and drove to the library on autopilot, her mind miles away from homework. As she passed the street Hank had indicated as the one on which the arrest was to have been made that morning, PJ decided to drive down it.

What she hoped to accomplish, she didn't know.

Someone had tapped into another person's personal router to conduct the hacking. That someone would have had to be close enough for the connection to work.

As she neared the end of the street, she slowed to turn onto the next one, glancing in her rearview mirror to make sure no one was following her, paranoia a given since the attack in her apartment.

A movement near the corner of a house caught PJ's eye and she inched onto the next street, her gaze flipping between the road in front of her and the street behind.

A young man in a T-shirt and baggy jeans slipped between houses, crossed the street and passed by the house with the stolen bandwidth.

The person was headed the same direction as PJ, so she slowed more, thankful traffic was so light in the small town during the middle of the day. As she neared the turn for the next street, the man crossed that road and walked between two more houses, head down, hands jammed into his pockets.

PJ turned and hurried toward the spot where the man had disappeared. She noted a fence blocking access to the backs of the houses. A driveway led to a garage with what appeared to be an apartment over the top.

Thinking she'd lost him, PJ rolled down her window and listened while she scanned the area. She almost missed the soft click of a door closing at the top of the stairs leading into the garage apartment.

She drove by and rounded the corner to the next

street, parking in the driveway of a vacant house with a For Sale sign jammed into the dry grass.

Her heart hammering, PJ checked all around for anyone following her before she opened her door and got out. Not a single vehicle passed on the street. The sun beat down on her, making her glad she'd opted for a ribbed knit T-shirt and khaki shorts. She grabbed a ball cap from the backseat, shoved her hair up into it and slid her sunglasses over her eyes. Then she took off along the sidewalk leading to the house with the garage apartment, stopping at the front door of the main house and quickly making up a story before she knocked.

An old woman answered, squinting through the screen door. PJ recognized her as one of the ladies who came into the diner maybe once every six months—Mrs. Grissom, if she recalled.

"Hello, I'm PJ Franks. I work at Cara Jo's Diner. I notice you have a garage apartment. Is it for rent?"

The woman's hand shook as she pushed the screen open to get a better look at PJ. "You're the waitress from the diner. I remember you."

"Yes, ma'am." PJ smiled.

"I'm sorry, but the apartment is already rented out to Bergman's grandson."

"Mr. Bergman, the hardware store owner?"

"That's him." The woman snorted. "Wouldn't have rented it to Ross, except I like his grandfather. Been wonderin' what he's been up to, but I don't get up those stairs often. The man has a bad attitude, and he's rude. Sheriff was by earlier lookin' for him. Probably up to no good."

"The sheriff?" PJ forced a smile, while her insides churned.

"Asked if I knew anything about Ross using computers or some such." The woman waved her hand. "I don't know anything about computers and, like I said, I haven't been up those stairs in a couple months."

All PJ heard was that the sheriff had been there looking for Ross with questions about computers. She sucked in a steadying breath and gave the old woman another smile to say that the world didn't hinge on Ross's computer abilities. "Oh, well, I hope it all works out with Mr. Bergman's grandson. And let me know if the apartment becomes available anytime soon. You know where to find me—at the diner."

"I sure do. Don't get there often, but I'll let you know." The old woman closed the screen door and the front door before PJ left the stoop.

Instead of going back to her car, PJ walked farther along the street until she was out of view of the windows from the upstairs apartment. Then she ducked between houses into the alleyway behind the buildings. A gate stood ajar, leading to the back of the garage apartment. Just inside the gate, a trash can stood against the fence. It was overflowing with garbage, and the lid was half-open.

With a quick glance at the staircase leading up

the side of the garage, PJ carefully lifted the lid and poked around.

If Ross made a daily trek through the neighborhoods, maybe he had something to do with hijacking the Wi-Fi capability. He could be the one hacking into Hank's computers. Who would have thought a small-town kid would know so much about computers? But was he also the man who'd broken into her apartment, attacked her and scared her by stealing her baby monitor? He was the right size and build.

Maybe there was a clue in his trash. PJ dug around an old pizza box and several soda bottles. When she encountered a cardboard box with a picture of a video camera on it, just like the miniature cameras they'd found in the day care and in her apartment, her hand shook and she almost dropped the evidence.

"Oh, my God." Her gaze shot to the door above. Nothing moved. PJ flattened the cardboard box and slid it under her shirt, and then she lowered the trash can lid and stepped toward the gate.

As she slipped through, she cast a glance back at the apartment in time to see the door opening.

Her heart in her throat, PJ ducked behind the fence and crouched in case Ross could see over the top of the wooden slats. If she kept still, he wouldn't know she was there.

Footsteps sounded on the steps and crunched across the gravel toward her. This guy who'd potentially hacked Hank's database might also be the guy who'd attacked her in her apartment, plus the other time to get a cheek swab. He was strong enough to easily overpower her and finish her off.

PJ debated making a run for it but decided to stay put. What reason would Ross have to go out the back gate?

The lid to the trash can opened, and the sound of cardboard hitting gravel gave PJ a start.

A man's muttered curse sounded as if next to her.

PJ held her breath and prayed he'd leave soon so she could get the hell out of there without being spotted.

The gravel crunched on the other side of the fence, and footsteps moved away from her.

About to let go of the breath she'd been holding, PJ stopped dead still when the cell phone she'd jammed into her back pocket rang.

Without waiting to see if Ross had heard and come looking for the source, PJ made a run for it, away from her car.

"Hey!" someone shouted behind her.

She ducked between two houses. A dog barked, racing along the side of a chain-link fence as she ran by.

Her lungs burned with each breath she inhaled, and she thought she might pass out before she circled back to her car. PJ held on to the tattered remains of the video camera box and ran as fast as she could, telling herself she'd been a fool to risk her life when she had a baby at home to protect. After rounding the corner by the next house, she dared to look back over her shoulder.

Nothing moved except the dog, still running back and forth along the fence.

PJ couldn't have heard pounding footsteps over the animal's barking and her own pulse in her ears. She dived behind a bush and squatted low to the ground, trying to catch her breath. After a while, the dog stopped barking and PJ dared to part the branches to peer out.

She couldn't see past the driveway, but she heard footsteps on pavement, running toward her from the other end of the house.

PJ cowered lower, her ragged breaths caught in her throat. Through the tiny window through the leaves, she saw Ross Felton running by.

He stopped in the middle of the street and spun in a 360-degree circle before jogging within a foot of the spot where she crouched, hidden by the bush.

The dog commenced barking, the sound moving away from her, back in the direction she'd just come from.

PJ crawled from behind the bush and edged close to the house. The dog was at the corner of his yard farthest away from PJ. Ross Felton was nowhere to be seen.

She inched back around the house and stood, brushed herself off and jogged back to her car, glancing over her shoulder every step of the way. Once she got into her car, cranked the engine and shifted into Drive, PJ finally allowed herself to breathe.

She wasn't cut out to be a spy, and she vowed never to do that again. After the scare with Ross, all she wanted to do was get home to Charlie.

When she pulled into the parking lot behind the resort, Chuck's truck was there and Dana's car was gone.

Great. Chuck would be mad she'd left the diner and even madder when he found out what she'd been doing. But damn it, he hadn't bothered to come fill her in on what was going on. He might be angry, but she had a bone to pick with him, as well.

Straightening her shoulders, she got out of the car and climbed the steps to her apartment.

Chuck opened the door before she could get her key in the lock.

With an excuse poised on her lips, she didn't get a chance to say anything before Chuck pulled her through the door and into his arms.

"Thank God you're home. I was worried when you didn't answer your phone."

Too late, PJ remembered the call that had triggered her headlong rush to get the hell away from Ross Felton's apartment. She would have laughed if she wasn't so busy kissing Chuck.

Her hands wound around the back of his neck, and she gave him her lips, hungry for contact with this big man who'd managed to turn her world inside out every time they were together.

When he finally set her at arm's length, he demanded, "Where have you been?"

PJ pulled the cardboard box out from beneath her shirt and handed it to Chuck. "Is this the same kind of video camera you found in the day care and here in my apartment?"

He took the box from her and frowned down at it. "Yes, it is. Where did you get it?"

"I found it in Ross Felton's trash can."

Chuck closed his eyes and drew in a deep breath. "How did you find out about Ross?"

PJ stepped out of his embrace. "Since no one bothered to call or let me know what was going on, I stopped by the sheriff's office. They told me someone had hacked the IP address. I just happened to drive down that street when I saw Ross Felton ducking through the houses."

Chuck gripped her arm with his empty hand. "Please tell me you didn't go to his apartment."

PJ shrugged. "Okay, I won't. But then I'd have a tough time explaining how I got this." She tapped the box he still held. "Don't worry. It wasn't in his apartment. I found it in his trash outside." She didn't tell him that Ross had almost caught her, or that she'd had to run from him to get away. Since the incident had ended well, that little bit of information was not necessary.

Chuck let go of her and ran his hand through his hair. "Woman, you have no idea how badly I want to shake you."

PJ grinned. "Don't worry. That's not something I'll ever do again. I'll leave spying up to the professionals." She looked around him. "Where's Charlie?"

"Napping in her crib. Dana left fifteen minutes ago. I need you to pack a bag."

"Why?" PJ stared up into his face.

The lines across his forehead and around his eyes seemed deeper.

"I'll explain when we're safely on the road to Hank's."

"I take it we're staying the night there," she stated.

"Right." Chuck refused to tell her anything more until they were in his truck and on their way out to the Raging Bull Ranch.

When he did fill her in on the blackmail note, PJ sat back against her seat and shook her head. "You think it's Ross who sent that note?"

"I'd say whoever it is might be getting desperate. With the sheriff looking for him and Hank's computer guy getting closer to tracking his hacking trail, he's running out of options."

"Why not just ignore the threat? So what if he tells the drug lords anything? Hell, we still don't know who my father is. Why would they care? How could his threat make things any worse than they already are?"

Chuck's fingers tightened on the steering wheel. "Because they can. The Mexican cartels have a far-reaching influence. If they decide you're a worthy target…"

"Great." PJ stared out the window at the road in front of her. The sun shone through the side window on its slow descent to the horizon. "Chuck, I don't know about you, but I'm tired of this."

AFTER A DELICIOUS dinner Hank's housekeeper had prepared but that PJ had barely touched, she fed Charlie and rocked her to sleep.

When she had Charlie settled in the crib in the bedroom she'd used the last time she'd stayed at Hank's, PJ headed back to the living room for answers.

Chuck and Hank stood by the window, staring out at the stars.

"Now that Charlie is asleep, perhaps you two could tell me why someone thinks he can blackmail Hank to keep from telling the drug lords who I am? Why is it a big deal? I'm just PJ Franks, not a celebrity, secret princess or someone special."

Hank faced her, a hint of a smile turning his lips upward. "You're special to me."

"No offense, Hank. But we barely know each other." PJ shoved her hands into her jeans pockets. "Does your blackmailer think this Mexican Mafia man will come after me? After all these years?" She shook her head. "It's hardly likely."

"Are you so confident that you'd stake Charlie's life on that?"

PJ's lips clamped shut, and she fought the urge to run to the bedroom where Charlie was sleeping, just to verify the baby was still there. "No. But it's insane to think a man can carry a grudge for that long." Her gaze slipped to Chuck in time to see him flinch. Perhaps her statement had hit too close to home in the case of his grudge with his own father.

"Still, PJ," Hank said, "I feel better knowing you're safe under my roof for the time being."

"I can't live here forever." PJ sighed. "I have a job and school."

"You have Charlie's safety and well-being to consider," Chuck argued.

"And I want to be able to support her and set a good example for her to follow by holding down a job and furthering my education. I can't run scared for an extended period of time. If we think Ross was the hacker, why hasn't the sheriff hauled him in for questioning?"

Hank shook his head. "They haven't caught up to him yet."

PJ's jaw tightened. "I should have called the sheriff instead of running," she muttered.

Chuck frowned. "What was that?"

She glanced up with a fake smile. "Nothing."

His frown deepened, but he didn't dig further.

PJ blew out a breath, thankful for the reprieve. She'd had enough drama for the day without explaining the wild chase scene to Chuck and Hank.

Running footsteps sounded on the Saltillo tiles.

Brandon skidded around the door frame into the living room, waving a computer tablet. "Got something you might be interested in," he said, breathing hard.

Hank frowned. "What is it?"

Brandon pressed the screen and handed the tablet to Hank. "Emilio Montalvo was spotted going through a border checkpoint under an assumed name and passport."

Chuck and PJ crossed the floor to where Hank stood and leaned over his shoulder, studying the photo. It was a grainy likeness of a Hispanic man wearing a business suit.

A twinge of recognition flitted across PJ's consciousness, but she couldn't put her finger on who Emilio reminded her of. "I take it Montalvo means bad news."

"The worst. Emilio Montalvo is a Mafia drug lord." Hank sucked in a breath. "He's my nemesis, and the man I mentioned who'd obsessed over PJ's mother."

The blood rushed from PJ's head, and she swayed where she was standing. "This Montalvo guy... could he be my father?"

Chapter Fifteen

Chuck stared across at PJ, whose face had gone completely white. He hurried over to her and slipped his arm around her waist, steadying her.

"Are you sure?" PJ shook her head. "Can't tell much from that photo."

Brandon reached between PJ and Chuck. "May I?"

Hank handed him the tablet, and Brandon tapped the screen several times and then handed it back to Hank. "That's the most current photo the DEA has on Montalvo."

The photo displayed a dark-haired, even darker-eyed Hispanic man, perhaps in his late forties or early fifties, with gray peppering his hair in natural streaks. He wore a light gray business suit and was standing in front of a building in what looked like a crowded business section of a city.

"That photo was taken two years ago in Mexico City," Brandon said. "Montalvo is influential in the government, having paid off every top official, and he has command of the largest cartel in all of Mexico. He's said to have amassed a fortune to rival Gates."

"That's my legacy?" PJ snorted. "A rich thug?" She shoved a hand through her hair, a smile hovering on her lips. "I don't know whether to laugh or cry."

"I wouldn't laugh." Hank stared across at PJ. "With that kind of money at his disposal, he can do just about anything he pleases or hire someone who can."

"You're not saying it, but I take it he could hire men to kill or kidnap me or Charlie."

"That and more. He can afford to hire an entire army if he wanted to."

"And he has. He funds the cartel activities along the border, and he has links in Puerto Rico, Dominican Republic, Cuba and along the entire East Coast of the U.S. He can smuggle any amount of drugs through his fronts, and all the government organizations in the U.S. arsenal haven't been able to stop him."

PJ leaned closer. "He looks familiar."

"If he is your father, you look nothing like him," Chuck said.

Where Montalvo had bushy black eyebrows and thick wavy black hair turning gray around the temples, PJ's was a light, sandy blond, straight and fine.

PJ touched her hair. "I look like my mother." She cast a glance at Chuck. "You saw the photo before it was stolen."

Chuck nodded. "You're as beautiful as she was."

PJ's gaze locked with his.

For a long moment, they might as well have been the only two people in the room. Chuck could practically feel the strength of PJ's emotions at the mention of her mother and the lost photo. He wanted to take her into his arms and hold her until that hurt look disappeared from her face.

"Any news on which way Montalvo is headed?" Chuck asked, knowing the answer but hopeful that he was wrong.

Brandon shook his head. "No, but we do have an image taken at the border of the vehicle he's traveling in. It's a full-size black SUV with heavily tinted windows and a Mexican license plate."

Hank handed the tablet to PJ and turned to Brandon. "Send that information to the sheriff's department. Ask Deputy Owen to put out a general alert to be on the lookout for the vehicle and to notify me if they spot it in or around Wild Oak Canyon."

PJ stared at the man in the photograph.

Chuck pulled her against him. "Don't worry. I'm here for you and Charlie."

She leaned into his body, resting her head against his chest. "Thanks." PJ continued to stare at the picture as if memorizing the man's features. "I can see how my mother might have fallen for him. He's not bad-looking. In fact, he's rather handsome. I could swear I've seen him before."

Chuck's hand tightened around her hip. "I had the same feeling."

She laughed. "To think, I always wanted a father. And now I might actually come face-to-face with him." She glanced across at Hank.

Hank stood with his hands in his pockets. "Not the best introduction to a man you didn't even know existed. Either way the DNA falls, huh?" He sighed. "I'm sorry, PJ. If I could undo the past, I would."

PJ smiled at him. "It's not your fault. Look how much you've done already, and I might not even be your daughter." She rubbed her arms. "I'll be glad to get the DNA results to settle the matter once and for all."

"I almost don't want to know." Hank sighed. "I like thinking you're my daughter. If the results come back that you aren't..."

Chuck could only imagine what it was like to be PJ, torn between wanting to know who her father was and fear of disappointment if he turned out to be a murdering drug lord.

Chuck's father hadn't been around much, but he'd made his mark on Chuck and his brother by his example. If not for the disagreement over Chuck's school choice, he could have claimed a normal childhood, filled with good moments as well as some not so good. He could still remember playing catch with the football when his father was home from deployments or overseas temporary-duty assignments.

On rare occasions, they'd gone camping as a family, his father teaching him and his brother how to start a fire without matches, how to make a shelter from limbs and branches and how to fish in a creek without a pole or hook. He'd treasured those moments. They'd made him the self-reliant man he was today.

PJ didn't have memories of her father and barely any of her mother.

Chuck's jaw tightened with his resolve to give Charlie memories she'd cherish. To be around for all those moments when a young girl needs a man to lean on.

"Any word on Ross Felton?" PJ asked. "Did the sheriff pull him in for questioning?"

Hank shook his head. "I called half an hour ago. Still nothing. They obtained a search warrant on his apartment. Apparently, he got wind of it and cleaned out his computers and files and ran with them."

"I guess there's not much more we can do then." PJ stepped away.

Chuck already missed the warmth of her body against his. "Might as well get some rest."

PJ nodded, her gaze locking with his.

Chuck couldn't read into her thoughts, whether she wanted him with her that night or not. He let her go to her room without him.

"She's very brave to have gone to Ross's apartment alone," Hank commented after PJ left.

"I can't believe she did. Alone." Chuck shoved a hand through his hair and paced the length of the living room. "I don't know if I can provide the protection she needs. The woman has a mind of her own."

Hank chuckled. "That she does. Much like her mother. Leaving a man of such influence in her country had to take a will of iron. To this day, I don't know how I let Alana go."

Chuck's gaze strayed to the hallway PJ had disappeared down. "I don't know how you let her go, either." He straightened his shoulders and steeled his resolve. "I'm not going to let go of PJ without a fight."

"I'm glad to hear that. You two belong together."

"I agree." Chuck cast a glance at Hank. "If you'll excuse me, I need to go convince *her*."

Hank's chuckle echoed behind him as Chuck strode down the hallway to PJ's room. He knocked and then pushed the door open. "PJ, we need to talk—"

"Okay, close the door and we'll talk." PJ stood by the bed, stripped her clothes off and held a soft white T-shirt against her front, covering little of her nakedness. "Well?"

"Sorry." Heat burned a path from Chuck's groin up his body into his cheeks. "I could just wait outside until you're finished."

PJ shook her head, tossed the T-shirt onto the bed and advanced across the floor. "Don't go."

Chuck couldn't move. His feet felt glued to the

floor, his gaze on the woman who'd stolen his heart more than three years ago.

Her body glowed in the soft light from the bedside lamp, her skin like pale cream, her curves fuller than before she'd had Charlie.

Chuck's gut clenched, his groin tightened and he finally stepped out of the doorway, closed it firmly behind him and twisted the lock. Then he gathered PJ in his arms, his hands sliding over her shoulders and along her sides, skimming the narrow arch of her waist to the flare of her hips. When he reached her thighs, he scooped her up, wrapping her legs around his waist.

"What was it you were saying about talking?" She cupped his face and lowered her lips to his.

"We need to…" Chuck couldn't wrap his mind around coherent thoughts when she was naked, her bare breasts pressing against his chest.

"Yes." Her lips claimed his in an urgent summons. "We do."

He carried her to the bed and laid her among the sheets, and then he straightened to feast his senses on PJ, his heart pounding against his ribs, his blood burning like fire through his veins.

Her long sandy-blond hair splayed out in a fan around her head. Her cheeks flushed a rosy pink, and she reached out. "Hurry."

Chuck ripped his shirt over his head, shucked his boots and jeans and moved between her legs. "You're even more beautiful than I remembered."

"Enough talk. I want you inside me. Now."

When he didn't move immediately, she frowned and sat up, her legs dangling over the side of the mattress. PJ wrapped her arms around his waist, and she kissed his belly. "Don't you want me?"

"You have no idea how badly I want you." Chuck disengaged her arms from around his waist and dropped to his knees in front of her. "But I want you to want me as badly."

"I don't think that will be a problem." She feathered her fingers through his hair and sighed. "What are we going to do about us?"

"This, for starters." He pressed his lips to the inside of her thigh.

"Mmm." PJ's fingers tugged at his hair. "Good start, cowboy."

"That's just the beginning." He licked and nipped a path, slowly moving toward her core.

As he touched his tongue to her center, PJ fell back against the bed, her fingers convulsing in the sheets, her back arching off the mattress. "Oh, please," she begged.

Chuck's chest rumbled with a chuckle he couldn't contain. His mouth left her briefly as a surge of passion fueled the joy he felt in that moment.

She half rose from the bed. "For Pete's sake, don't stop now," she moaned.

Bending to the task, he parted her folds and flicked that nubbin in the middle.

Her body grew rigid with each touch.

Lust powered through him, urging him to rise and take her, to drive deep inside her warm, wet channel. Chuck resisted, knowing PJ was close. He wanted her to feel everything as intensely as he did when he finally thrust into her. With a tenuous grip on his own excitement, he stroked and coaxed until her body grew rigid and her heels dug into his shoulders.

Chuck pushed to his feet and wrapped PJ's legs around his waist, thrusting deeply into her warmth.

Rocked by the force of their passion, PJ tightened her legs around Chuck, urging him to pump faster, to drive deeper and fill all the emptiness she'd endured for the past year. As they catapulted over the edge together, she knew in that startlingly clear instant that she could not send this man away ever again. She needed him in her life. He made her feel complete.

As she drifted back to earth in a warm haze of contentment, she guided him up beside her on the bed, refusing to lose their intimate connection.

With so many thoughts in her head swirling around, needing to be voiced, she couldn't think past Chuck's arms around her, holding her close, or his body enveloping hers in his strength.

The craziness of the day faded in the security of Chuck's arms, and PJ slipped into a deep sleep, nestled against the broad expanse of his chest. They could talk in the morning. First thing.

In the darkness of the night, Chuck stirred beside her, slipping from the bed. He drew the blanket up around her shoulders and pressed a kiss to her forehead.

PJ's eyes opened. "Where are you going?"

"I need to check on something."

"I'll come with you."

"I shouldn't be long. You need your sleep. Charlie will be waking early and needing her mother."

"Don't go far. I need you, too." PJ drifted back into a deep sleep, dreaming of a house with a picket fence and a yard that Charlie could play in.

Chuck strode through the gate, a cowboy hat tipped forward, that sexy swagger making PJ's heart stutter.

CHUCK STEPPED INTO his jeans and slipped into the hallway, carrying his shirt and boots. He met Hank in the living room.

"I'm sorry to wake you at this hour, but the sheriff's department called. They spotted two dark SUVs meeting the description Brandon sent them."

"Did they stop them?"

"They don't have any probable cause."

Frustration burned in Chuck's gut. "What can we do?"

"Nothing for now. I thought you'd want to know."

Chuck nodded. "All the more reason to stay close to PJ."

"Right. I've notified my security team, as well."

"Sheriff have anything on Ross?"

"Nothing. He seems to have made a clean get-away. Oh, and Mrs. Grissom told them Ross owns a black motorcycle."

Chuck's lips tightened. He hated inaction.

Hank tipped his head toward the door. "You might as well get some sleep. The night shift is competent, and the security cameras are back online."

"Thanks for letting me know."

"Just take care of PJ and Charlie."

Chuck returned to the bedroom, removed his boots and shirt and lay down on top of the covers beside PJ.

She turned toward him and snuggled against him, her hand resting on his chest, her eyes closed in sleep.

What Chuck wouldn't give to freeze this moment in time, to always be with PJ and Charlie. They had so much to talk about.

He lay for a long time staring up at the ceiling, planning what he'd say to PJ when she woke. He'd tell her he never stopped loving her and that they belonged together. Whatever she wanted from him, he'd give. If she wanted him to stay in Wild Oak Canyon and take a job that kept him close to home, so be it. He wanted to be a husband and father, to build a life for the three of them.

And after seven long years, he'd do something about the rift in his own family. Seven years was a long time to hold a grudge. He and his father had had more good times than bad. That should count for something. All that was needed was someone to take the first step.

The more he thought about it, the more excited he became about seeing his brother, sister, mother and even his dad.

Morning couldn't come soon enough.

He must have drifted off to sleep somewhere around two in the morning.

The next thing he knew, an enormous boom rocked the bed and threw him onto the floor.

Chapter Sixteen

Her ears ringing, PJ jerked upright in the bed. "Chuck?"

A groan sounded from the other side, and she heard a muttered, "What the hell?"

"Chuck?" PJ scrambled to her feet, wrapping a sheet around her naked body. She swayed, blinking the sleep from her eyes. "What was that?"

"I don't know." He rose to his feet. "Stay put until I figure it out." Chuck jammed his boots on his feet and threw open the French doors.

Charlie whimpered in her crib. PJ gathered her in her arms and followed Chuck to the door.

Outside, the night sky was lit up like daylight, a two-story blaze ripping toward the sky from where one of the outbuildings had once stood.

"Damn." Chuck faced PJ. "You should be all right in the house, but that fire is getting really close to the barn and horses."

"Go. Get those horses out before they burn." She glanced at Charlie and back to Chuck. "We'll be okay. I'll keep watch in case the fire spreads."

Chuck cupped her cheeks between his palms and kissed her. "I'll be back as soon as possible."

She smiled and kissed him back. "I know."

Before he left, he ran down the hallway and returned with one of Hank's security guards, who he posted outside the bedroom door. "He's going to watch out for you two while I'm outside. Yell if you need him. And try not to give him any trouble." Chuck winked, kissed her again and took off toward the barn, where several more of Hank's security guards and his foreman had converged.

Charlie turned her face toward PJ.

PJ laughed. "The world's on fire and you're hungry." She pulled the sheet off her breast and let Charlie nurse, all the while feeling as if she could be doing more.

PJ reminded herself that Charlie's well-being was her sole responsibility.

When Charlie had nursed for several minutes, she slipped back into a deep sleep, tummy full, cheeks still moving in a sucking motion.

PJ leaned her over her shoulder and patted a burp out of her before laying her back in her crib and hurrying to dress in case they had to leave quickly. She flipped the light switch on the wall, and nothing happened.

Apparently the explosion had knocked the electricity out. PJ moved around in the dark, rescuing her clothes from the floor where they'd fallen earlier that night.

After dressing, she stood staring out the windows of the French door, the scent of smoke seeping through the cracks every time the wind shifted. If it got much worse, she'd have to move Charlie deeper into the house.

A shout rose from one of the men racing around the barnyard. Flames rose from his arm where his shirt had caught fire.

PJ's breath caught. She pushed the French door open and stepped out onto the porch, debating whether she should help or stay put. Silhouetted against the inferno of the burning outbuilding, the man's face was hidden in dark shadows.

For all PJ knew, it could be Chuck.

She ran along the porch and down the steps toward the barnyard. Before she reached the bottom, another man emerged from the smoke, tackled the burning man and smothered the flames.

PJ waited until the men on the ground both stood, and then she released the breath she'd been holding.

When she turned back toward the house, she frowned.

She could have sworn she'd left the French door to her bedroom open.

Perhaps the wind had blown it closed. Only the wind wasn't blowing at that moment.

PJ hurried back to the door and reached for the knob.

It wouldn't turn.

She twisted it harder. Still it wouldn't open. Her

heart hammering against her chest, the flames rising higher behind her, PJ panicked and ran for the front of the ranch house.

The enormous double doors stood open, the interior cast in shadows. With the electricity out, PJ could only feel her way across the foyer, dependent on the light edging through some of the windows from the fire outside.

Her pulse pounding against her eardrums, she fought to remember how many doors had been before hers on the long, dark hallway. She counted two and flung open the third. The fire's blaze lit up the room through the open curtains. It wasn't the right one.

She backed into the hallway and moved to the next room. When she tried the door, it was locked. Too late, she remembered Chuck locking it the night before. Back down the hallway, she ran out onto the deck. Charlie was alone in the locked room. If the fire spread to the house...

PJ couldn't bear thinking about the consequences. She might not have the strength to open a locked wooden door, but she sure as hell could break a window in the French door.

Back around the side of the house, she ran, arriving in front of the French door. She leaned back and jammed her heel into the glass near the door handle.

It cracked but held.

Again, she kicked the glass. This time it broke, the shards falling inside. Careful not to cut herself,

she stuck her hand through the broken glass, un-
locked the French door and ran inside. "Charlie,
baby, Mommy's back."

She hurried to the crib and bent over to gather
her daughter into her arms.

Only Charlie wasn't there.

A plain white envelope lay against the crib sheet,
barely visible in the light streaming through the
open French door.

Her heart thudding against her ribs, PJ snatched
the envelope from the sheet and ripped it open. She
read the words by the light of the fire's blaze:

If you want to see your baby again, be at the barn
on the old Frisco Ranch at 3:00 a.m. Come alone
and tell no one. If you bring anyone with you, your
baby will disappear forever.

Tears spilled onto the paper, blurring the ink. PJ's
first instinct was to run to Chuck and beg him to
help her get her daughter back.

How could she get to the barn when her car was
back at her apartment? She didn't have Chuck's
truck keys, and she couldn't ask Hank's employees
to give her a lift without raising questions.

She grabbed her purse, pulled out her cell phone
and clicked it on. The clock indicated she had less
than an hour to get where she needed to be. She
was vaguely familiar with the location of the Frisco
Ranch. It had been abandoned three years earlier

when the old man who'd owned it died and his relatives had put it up for sale. No one had lived there since, as far as PJ knew.

If she could get to her apartment, she had the nine-millimeter pistol in her closet, the one she'd inherited from her adoptive mother when she'd passed.

She could call Dana for a ride, but Dana would ask too many questions PJ couldn't answer. And Dana wouldn't let her go alone to find Charlie. PJ wouldn't want her to follow because that would place her in danger, as well. No, she needed a taxi, someone who wouldn't ask questions, just pick her up and take her back to her apartment. Unfortunately, Wild Oak Canyon was fresh out of taxis, and her time was running out with each passing minute.

Then she remembered the card Señor Iglesias had insisted she take should she ever need anything. PJ had slipped it into her wallet and forgotten about it until now. Was he still at the resort? Would he pick up a call at this hour and take her back to the resort where she could collect her car?

PJ yanked her wallet from her purse, found the card and, using the light from the display screen of her phone, keyed in the number. She held her breath, praying for enough reception for the call to go through.

After a long, agonizing few seconds, the phone rang. And rang again.

After the fifth ring, PJ's hands trembled and she was on the verge of tears.

"Hola," a gravelly voice said.

"Oh, thank God," PJ breathed into the phone. "Mr. Iglesias, this is PJ Franks."

"Señorita Franks, *por favor,* what is wrong?"

Her voice shook. "I need a huge favor."

"Anything. You have but to ask."

Minutes later, PJ was racing down the long driveway toward the highway.

Sirens screamed in the distance, headed toward the Raging Bull Ranch.

PJ reached the highway and turned toward town, running until she got a stitch in her side.

The sirens were getting closer. PJ couldn't risk someone noticing her and trying to stop her from getting to her rendezvous. She ducked into the ditch and lay flat on the ground until first a paramedic truck raced by, and then a fire engine. All the while she lay against the dry Texas soil, she prayed for Charlie and Chuck and that there weren't any snakes or scorpions on the ground around her.

Once the rescue vehicles sped by, PJ was up and running again toward town. A lone set of headlights blinked into view. By the time the vehicle pulled up next to her on the highway, PJ couldn't take another step.

The window slid down and Señor Iglesias's kind face gazed out in concern. "Señorita Franks." He shifted into Park.

"Don't get out," PJ gasped between breaths. She ran around to the passenger seat and climbed in. "I need to get to my apartment as fast as you can go."

"What is going on?" His gaze rose to the sky lit up by the raging fire.

"A building exploded. Please, I need you to take me back to my apartment at the resort. Now."

"Sí." He turned the sleek black sedan in the middle of the road, bumping along the shoulder until he was aimed in the opposite direction. Once he had the vehicle straight, he pressed his foot to the floorboard, shooting them forward.

His hands gripped the steering wheel in a knuckle-white grip. "Perhaps you can tell me why we must break the speed laws?"

"I'm sorry, but no." She sat against the other side of the car, her thoughts on Charlie and what her baby was going through. She wouldn't understand what was happening. She wouldn't recognize her abductor. If she cried, would the kidnapper hurt her? PJ's heart squeezed so hard she could barely breathe. Now that she wasn't running, she had too much time to think.

"You are obviously distressed." The old man shot several glances at her, quick to return his attention to the road, which was speeding by at an alarming rate. "Is there anything I can do to help?"

"No." Her voice caught on a sob. She swallowed hard. "I just need to get to my apartment."

He sat quietly, concentrating on the road. When they neared town, he slowed.

PJ chewed the inside of her mouth to keep from urging him to go faster. They couldn't afford to be stopped by the law. She didn't have time to waste. She checked her cell phone. Less than thirty minutes remained.

Her stomach clenched as they neared the resort. "Please, drop me here."

Before he pulled to a complete stop at the corner of the diner, PJ flung open her door and jumped out. "Thank you, Señor Iglesias," she called out as she sprinted for the back of the building, clutching her keys in her hand. The motion-sensing lights blinked on, illuminating her way to the stairs. She ran up them two at a time, jamming the key into the lock when she reached the door.

She headed for the closet, pulling the ladies' shoe box down from the top shelf. The nine-millimeter pistol lay wrapped in a baby-blue winter scarf with a box of bullets beside it. She grabbed both, expelled the clip onto her bed and loaded it with bullets, fumbling twice, dropping ammunition on the coverlet.

When she had the clip full, she jammed it into the weapon, grabbed her keys and ran for the door.

Once in her car, she checked the time on her dash. Fifteen minutes to get there. She didn't have time for stop signs or speed limits. PJ flew through town, heading north on a farm-to-market road. She knew where the Frisco Ranch was only because she and her adopted mother, Terri Franks, had visited the old man when he'd been sick. That had been years ago. In the dark, with only the stars and a general idea to guide her, PJ was at a disadvantage. Several times she screeched to a halt—to peer through the gloom at a rickety gate, to read the name on an old mailbox and to hesitate at a faded dirt road leading off the highway. When she'd about given up hope, her headlights glanced off a wooden gate with the faded lettering written across the arch listing to the east: Frisco Ranch.

PJ swallowed the sob rising up her throat and turned onto the rutted road. Tire tracks pressed into the dust, indicating someone else had arrived before her.

"Charlie."

PJ pressed the accelerator, shooting the vehicle forward. Her little car bumped along, spewing a cloud of dust behind it, hitting bottom several times on the high center between the ruts.

Finally the old cabin came into view. PJ passed it by, heading straight for the rustic barn behind.

She almost cried when she didn't see any vehicles in front of the weathered building. PJ jammed the gun into the back of her pants and climbed out of the car, leaving the engine running and the headlights shining at the building.

"I'm here and I'm alone," she called out. "Where's my baby?"

Her voice echoed in the night sky.

For a long moment, nothing stirred and no one moved or came out from the shadows.

"Please," PJ sobbed. "Please don't hurt her."

"Shut up. No one's gonna hurt anyone." Ross Felton pushed the barn door open and stepped out, carrying a gun.

PJ peered around him, trying to see into the barn. She stepped forward.

Ross raised the pistol. "Stay where you are."

"Where's Charlie?"

"In the barn. She'll be fine as long as you do exactly as I say."

"Anything, just don't hurt my baby." PJ wrung her hands, wanting to pull out the gun and shoot the bastard for taking her baby, but afraid he'd do something to hurt Charlie if PJ missed. "What do you want?"

"I want you to shut up." He glanced over her shoulder. "Good, their timing is right on."

PJ looked behind her to see two pairs of headlights pulling into the barnyard.

Black SUVs parked beside her little car, and rough-looking men in dark clothing stepped down. One of them came forward. He had a scar across his face and tattoos across his arms and neck. He grabbed her from behind and pulled the gun from her waistband, and then he spun her away. He laughed and waved the gun at the others, speaking in rapid-fire Spanish.

The other men laughed.

PJ straightened, pushing back her fear. Charlie needed her to keep a level head and get the two of them out of this mess. "What do you want with me?"

The laughter died away, and another man stepped out from behind one of the SUVs.

PJ's breath caught. It was the man from the picture Brandon had shown her earlier. Emilio Montalvo.

"I wish to know my daughter and granddaughter," he said in heavily accented English.

With her heart plummeting, PJ held her head high. "And who might that be?" she stalled, afraid he knew more than she did about her lineage. Dear Lord, she wasn't ready to accept the truth.

His brows rose, and the corners of his mouth turned up. "You, *hija*."

Lead hit the pit of her belly, and she fought to keep a poker face. "I don't know what you're talking about."

Emilio nodded to Ross. "Tell her."

Ross licked his lips, his gaze darting between Emilio and PJ. "Your DNA results came back a match with his."

PJ's eyes narrowed, and she focused her anger on Ross. "You're the bastard who tied me up and left me behind the trash can."

Ross shrugged. "I needed the sample and didn't figure you'd give it willingly."

"So you've established who my biological father is. So what?" PJ crossed her arms over her chest to keep her hands from visibly shaking. "That means nothing to me."

"On the contrary. It means you are a Montalvo. You belong in Mexico with your family."

"My family is here. I'm not going anywhere."

"Oh, we will take your baby, as well. After all, she is a Montalvo, as well."

PJ was already shaking her head. "No."

Emilio's eyes darkened, and his brows dipped low. He stepped up to her and stared down his nose at her. "You deny your heritage?"

"I told you, my home is here. I'm not going anywhere with you."

His hand shot out, and he slapped her face so hard, she fell to the ground.

PJ's hand rose to her mouth where warm, red blood trickled from her lip onto her fingers. She pushed to her feet. "This is how you treat family? I understand why my mother ran away from you."

"Madre de Dios," he gritted out. He raised his hand to strike again.

PJ held her ground, refusing to back down from the man.

"No mas!" a voice cried out behind Emilio.

PJ glanced over Emilio's shoulder to the man

standing at the edge of the shadows, holding a gun pointed at her biological father.

"Señor Iglesias?" PJ shook her head, regret burning a hole in her gut. The man had followed her and now faced a firing squad of cartel members.

"Hit her again," Iglesias said in English, "and I will kill you."

Emilio laughed. "You do not have the stomach to kill your own son."

PJ stared at the older man, her jaw slack. "Son?"

Emilio turned back to PJ. "Ah, I see you have already met your grandfather."

ONCE THE FIRE trucks arrived, Chuck pulled away from the blaze and trudged back to the house to check on PJ and Charlie.

Before he reached the porch, Brandon raced up beside him. "Where's Hank?"

"With the fire chief." Chuck stopped in front of the younger man. "Why?"

"I know who did it. I know who set the explosion."

"Who?" He gripped Brandon's arms. "Who did this?"

"Ross Felton." He grinned. "Once I got the electricity on and the video monitoring system back online, I checked the last feed before the system went down to see if I could track what had happened. I noticed someone sneaking up on the corner of the outbuilding that exploded."

Chuck climbed the steps, pushing past Brandon. If Ross Felton had been on the Raging Bull Ranch...

As he crossed the decking, all the air left Chuck's lungs.

The glass in the French doors to the bedroom he'd shared with PJ was broken, and the door stood open.

Brandon followed. "Why is the door broken?"

Only half listening, Chuck entered the bedroom, crunching across shards of glass. "PJ?" The lights were on, but no one stirred in the room.

He hurried across to the crib and stared down, knowing before he saw it with his own eyes that Charlie wouldn't be there. Instinct told him they were gone, but he had to know for sure. "PJ?" he yelled, throwing open the door to the rest of the house. The guard he'd posted lay crumpled against the wall, a knot forming on his head. He checked for a pulse. "Call 9-1-1 and get this man some help."

"Will do," Brandon said.

Chuck raced along the corridors, searching each bedroom, the living room and the kitchen on the off chance she'd gone for a bite to eat, even though it didn't explain the broken glass or the unconscious guard.

"Mr. Bolton." Brandon emerged from the bedroom. "I found this." He held out a crumpled note. "It was on the floor beside the crib."

Chuck snatched the paper from his hands and read, the blood rushing out of his head, his hand tightening on the note until his knuckles turned white. Then he fisted the paper and threw it. "Get Hank. Now!"

Brandon ran for the door. He was back in less than a minute.

Chuck had returned to the bedroom to gather his gun and ammo. "I'm going after them."

"I'm coming with you," Hank said. "I've already put a call out for the other agents. They will meet us there. If we leave now, we can be there in thirty minutes."

"Thirty minutes is fifteen minutes after PJ was supposed to meet Felton at the barn. We might be too late."

"I'd suggest taking the helicopter, but we don't know if it was damaged in the explosion."

"We're wasting time." Chuck charged for the door.

Hank followed, shouting orders to his security guards. "In twenty minutes, notify the police. No sooner. If they get there before us, no telling what Felton will do. We can't risk PJ and Charlie's lives."

"Assuming Felton's our only problem." Chuck reached his truck first, leaping into the driver's seat. He shifted into Reverse a little harder than he should have, jamming his foot to the accelerator.

Hank pulled his seat belt across his chest and snapped it in place. "They'll be okay."

Chuck's jaw tightened. "I promised I'd take care of them."

"And you will," Hank reassured him.

Yeah, Chuck thought. *If we aren't already too late.*

Chapter Seventeen

PJ inched to the side, hoping to get out of the line of fire from Señor Iglesias's gun. If Emilio refused to back down, it would get ugly.

As soon as she moved, Emilio reached out and snagged her arm, yanking her in front of him. He jammed the barrel of a pistol into her temple. "You will have to shoot us both."

"Let her go, Emilio." Señor Iglesias stared from Emilio to PJ and back. "I am an excellent marksman."

"Por favor." Emilio stood still, calling the old man's bluff. "Gamble on your skills."

"Why would you kill her?"

"He took my Alana. Hank Derringer stole her from me. I will finally make him pay."

PJ's gaze caught a movement to her right. One of Emilio's goons had raised his weapon and was aiming it at Señor Iglesias. If PJ didn't do something quickly, he'd be shot.

She sucked in a breath, pulled her arm up to her chest and jammed it backward into Emilio's gut, ducking as soon as his arm loosened around her. "Run, Señor Iglesias!" she cried out and threw herself to the ground.

A shot rang out.

PJ scrambled to get her feet under her, but not fast enough.

Emilio grabbed her hair and dragged PJ to her knees. "You should not have done that, *hija*. Look what you have done." He jerked her head around. "You cost my father his life."

A sob rose up PJ's throat.

Lying on the ground in a pool of blood was Señor Iglesias.

"And so that you know, his name was Ricardo Iglesias *Montalvo*." Emilio flung her away from him. He nodded toward his men and spoke in Spanish.

With PJ's limited understanding of the language, she caught only a word or two. Something about *child* and *woman*. Two men moved toward the barn.

Ross Felton stood at the door. "You don't get the baby until I get my money."

Emilio snorted. "I will pay you when I get both the woman and the child."

"And I told you I wouldn't let you have both until I get paid."

Emilio's lip curled into a snarl, the look so evil it made PJ's gut clench and a chill slither down her spine.

In the blink of an eye, Emilio raised his gun and shot Ross through the heart.

The stunned look on Ross's face would have been comical had he not dropped to his knees in the next second, falling to his face in the dirt.

"No!" PJ lurched to her feet and ran for the barn. "Leave my baby alone!" she cried.

One man grabbed her as she tried to duck past him.

PJ was no match for his size and strength.

He jerked her arms behind her and held her effortlessly at arm's length while the other man entered the barn.

A few seconds later, PJ heard a curse.

The man emerged with a baby blanket and a child's doll. He threw them to the ground at Emilio's feet.

Emilio spoke to him in Spanish. Three men entered the barn.

PJ held her breath. Where was Charlie? Ross was the only one who had that answer, and he was dead. Her heart skipped several beats as a dozen different scenarios flitted through her head, each with a worse outcome than the last.

When the men emerged empty-handed, Emilio roared, crossed to Ross and kicked his lifeless body. He yelled at the men, "Look again!"

PJ positioned herself to run. If the men were occupied searching for Charlie, she could escape and come back to find the baby with some help. Assuming she could get back to town on foot without being spotted by Emilio and his gang. In the meantime, anything could happen to Charlie. If she was lying somewhere in the dark, an animal could hurt her; a snakebite would kill her.

She couldn't leave, not without Charlie.

Emilio returned to PJ and jerked her to her feet. "Where is the baby?"

PJ shook her head, convinced Charlie was better off lost than in the hands of these terrorists. "I don't know."

Emilio backhanded her.

This time PJ was ready. She ducked, the blow glancing off the side of her head. Just as quickly as he hit her, PJ kicked him hard in the groin.

The man doubled over and fell to the ground, his hand angling upward, the gun pointed at PJ.

PJ kicked again, sending the gun flying into the brush. Then she ran, knowing if she stayed, Emilio would kill her, daughter or not.

She made it two steps before Emilio grabbed her ankle.

PJ toppled to the ground, hitting her head so hard that her vision blurred and she teetered on the edge of passing out, gray fog creeping in around her.

Emilio crawled up her body, grabbed her hair and jerked her head back. "You will pay for that, *hija*."

A shot pierced the night.

Emilio jerked backward, his hand still wrapped around PJ's hair, flinging her with him.

PJ landed on her side, pain shooting through her temples. Blackness engulfed her, pulling her down into an abyss so deep, she could no longer resist.

"Charlie," she whispered as the darkness claimed her.

"I THINK SHE'S coming around." Katie's voice made Chuck raise his head from the back of the uncomfortable hospital chair where he'd fallen asleep holding Charlie. It had been two days since he'd found PJ at the Frisco Ranch. Two long days where she'd lain in the hospital bed, pale, listless and unconscious.

The doctor said she had a concussion but couldn't predict when she'd wake up. The stress of all she'd gone through plus the trauma to her head had done a number on her.

"Look, her eyes are twitching." Katie leaned over PJ's face.

Chuck couldn't get over how Katie had grown in the past seven years. At seventeen, she was a beautiful young woman with all the joy and exuberance of youth.

She glanced at him, a frown pulling her pretty brows together. "You're looking at me that way again. Stop."

"What way?"

"Like you're gonna hug me again." She grinned. "Not that I mind. It isn't every day your long-lost brother calls in the middle of the night." Her eyes welled. "You should have seen Mom's face."

Chuck stared down at the baby in his arms, imagining her refusing to return home because of something he'd said. He vowed never to say anything to drive her away. And he vowed never to let words drive a wedge between himself and his family again.

"Any change?" A woman's voice at the door brought Chuck's head up.

His mother smiled at him and entered, followed by his father.

His parents looked so much older than when he'd left. His father's hair, which had just a hint of gray seven years ago, had turned solid gray. The crow's feet around his mother's eyes had deepened, and the worry lines across her forehead were permanently etched into her skin. "Can I?" She reached for Charlie.

Chuck let her take the baby, and then he stood and stretched. "How long was I asleep?"

"All of twenty minutes. Mom said I couldn't wake you."

"We should go out to the waiting room." Sylvia Bolton hugged Charlie to her. "PJ needs her rest to get better."

Katie rolled her eyes. "She's unconscious, Mom. How much more restful can you be?"

Chuck snagged her around the waist and pulled her into his arms. "I missed you and your smart mouth."

"Yeah, I know." She hugged him back. "Don't ever ditch me again, you hear?"

"Yes, ma'am." He rubbed his knuckles across the top of her head as he had when she was ten.

"Hey, you're messin' up my hair."

"Then stop getting so pretty." Chuck patted her hair into place. "I bet Dad's been beating the boys off with a stick."

"No, but he polishes his rifle on the porch every time a date comes to pick me up. Talk to him, will ya? It's cramping my style." Katie headed for the door. "Come on, Mom, we can play with Charlie in the waiting room. It's crowded in here."

The two women exited, leaving Chuck alone with his father for the first time in seven years.

Daniel Bolton stood with his hands in his pockets, his gaze on PJ. "She must be something special."

"She is." At a loss for how to bridge the gap between himself and his father, Chuck stood on the other side of the bed, staring at the woman who'd changed his life forever. "I'd give my life for her and Charlie."

"I hear you almost did."

Chuck shrugged. "It could have gone bad just as easily." He and Hank had arrived at the Frisco Ranch a lot later than he'd wanted to, but driving with the lights out to keep from being detected too soon had been difficult with scattered clouds limiting the light from the moon and stars.

He and Hank had ditched his truck on the highway and gone on foot, in a parallel path to the driveway leading in. When they heard gunfire, they'd thrown caution to the wind and ran the remaining yards to the house.

The second shot rang out as they peered around the corner of the house. Ross Felton had toppled to the ground.

When Chuck saw Emilio yank PJ up by the hair, blood flushed over his eyes and the same feeling he'd gotten when he'd found the dead Afghan boy outside the compound almost took over.

But he'd learned his lesson. He couldn't go off half-cocked. He had to think, to plan, to make his next move count, or he could lose PJ forever.

He raised his pistol and aimed, his eyes lining up his sights. Then he'd fired, all in the space of a second. Emilio lay dead. PJ lay beside him in the dirt, unmoving.

Hank picked off the first of Emilio's men to emerge from the barn.

Chuck focused enough to take out the second. The third man came out with his hands up, tossing his weapon to the dirt.

The sheriff arrived within minutes, calling for the ambulance.

Then the desperate hunt began. It took every able-bodied person searching the entire ranch compound to locate Charlie. Just when they were about to give up, Hank found her.

Ross Felton had stashed her in a closet in the abandoned house. When he'd emerged from the house carrying a softly crying Charlie, Chuck had gathered his tiny daughter in his arms and cried with her.

They rode in the back of the ambulance to the hospital with PJ and had been there since.

"Thank you for calling when you did." Chuck's father broke through Chuck's thoughts, bringing him back to the hospital room and PJ's still body.

"I waited too long." Chuck shook his head. "I was too stubborn."

"No, I waited too long." His father sighed. "As soon as you left, I knew I was wrong. I wanted to call you back, but I was so angry. I wanted the world for you."

"I didn't want your world."

"I know that now." His father stared down at PJ. "I'm sorry."

Chuck nodded. "Me, too."

They stood silently on opposite sides of PJ's bed, the chasm between them narrowing.

Chuck felt as if a great weight had lifted from his heart. He couldn't wait for PJ to wake and share the joy with him.

"Hey." The soft sound of PJ's whisper tugged at Chuck's consciousness. At first he thought he'd imagined it.

Then PJ's eyes blinked open. She stared up at him and raised her hand to shield her eyes. "Charlie?"

"Is fine. She's with my mother and sister in the waiting room."

She turned to the other man smiling down at her. "You must be Chuck's dad."

He chuckled. "How'd you guess?"

"You look so much alike."

Chuck stared at his father, and his father stared back.

"It's been said we're a lot alike," the older Bolton said.

"Then we'll get along just fine, seeing as I love your son." Her voice trailed off, and her eyes closed.

Chuck clutched her hand, his throat tight, his eyes stinging with unshed tears. "PJ?"

"I'm here," she said. "I'd open my eyes, but that light is really bright."

Chuck's dad crossed to the light switch and flipped it off. "I'll let the doc know she's awake." He slipped from the room, leaving them alone.

Chuck pressed his lips to PJ's forehead. "You had me scared."

"Think I'd go off and leave you to take care of Charlie on your own?"

He chuckled. "Something like that."

"Don't worry. I'm not going anywhere."

"And neither am I. If you'll have me."

"Chuck?"

"Yeah, baby?"

"I meant what I said to your father."

"That we look alike?"

"Not that." She opened her eyes and stared up into his, her hand tightening around his. "I love you.

There, I said it. I can't take it back and wouldn't if I could."

"I've always loved you, PJ. You're what kept me sane in the sandbox. The thought of seeing you again made me want to go on living."

"I was wrong to push you away. You have to take love any way you can get it." She pressed his hand to her cheek. "If you want to go off to war and defend our country, I'll be here when you get back. I'll take any time you give me. Just come back when you're done. Charlie and I will be waiting."

"I'm done with the army."

"What about Hank's team?"

"I like what he stands for. I want to continue working for him. But if it makes you uncomfortable, I'll go to work at the local feed store or hire on as the stable hand at the resort. I hear they need a permanent replacement for the one who quit." He smiled.

"No. Work for Hank. He's a good man. I'll take whatever love I can get for as long as I have it." She pulled him close and brushed her lips across his, wincing. "Ouch."

Chuck frowned, touching her cheek with his thumb. "You have a bruised lip."

"Emilio." Her eyes widened. "Is he—"

Chuck nodded. "Dead."

"Ricardo?"

A smile tilted the corners of his lips. "He was airlifted to the hospital in El Paso and is in intensive care, but the prognosis is good."

"I'm glad." PJ sighed. "He tried to save me. How did he know where to find me?"

"He said he'd had a team of computer hackers following Emilio's communications. He intercepted the emails from Ross and wanted to see for himself the granddaughter he'd never known. And never will."

Chuck was about to kiss PJ again, but a soft tap on the door interrupted.

Hank Derringer poked his head inside. "I hear she's—" His gaze landed on PJ. "Hey, you're awake."

"I am." She held up a hand.

Hank crossed the room and took her hand in his. "I'm glad you're doing better. You had us all worried."

"Thanks for hiring Chuck to protect me."

"Only the best for my girl." He leaned over and kissed her forehead.

PJ blinked up at him, her eyes clouding. "Only I'm not your daughter. Ross and Emilio told me." She smiled, her bottom lip trembling. "Guess it wasn't meant to be."

Hank frowned. "What are you talking about?" He laid his hand on her forehead. "Is she still hallucinating?"

Chuck laughed. "She better not be. She told me she loved me."

Hank grinned and pulled a sheet of paper from his pocket. "In that case, I'll leave this with you."

Chuck took the paper and spread it out on the bed beside PJ.

"It's the results of the DNA test." Hank's smile broadened. "I'm afraid you're stuck with me, PJ."

"But Ross said—"

"He lied. Brandon hacked his computer and found out what Ross had been up to through a series of emails he'd sent to Emilio. When Ross broke into Hank's computer, he discovered Hank's ongoing investigation of Emilio, as well as PJ's connection. He sold the information to Emilio, making him believe PJ was his daughter and Charlie was his granddaughter. Emilio demanded a DNA test to prove it."

"And?"

"Brandon found the email with the DNA results of the test he conducted on you and Emilio. You weren't a match."

"You're my father?" Her lips spread, followed quickly by a grimace. "I have a father." She looked up at him. "I'd smile, but it hurts."

Hank patted her hand. "Don't worry. You'll have plenty of opportunities to smile. And if you can stand being around an old guy, I want you and Charlie to come live with me."

PJ glanced from Hank to Chuck.

Chuck shook his head. "Sorry, Hank. PJ's all grown up and getting married soon."

Her eyes widened. "I am?"

He kissed her fingertips. "If you'll say yes."

She smiled, winced and smiled again. "Yes!"

Hank chuckled. "I'll leave you to it, but I want you to visit often. Chuck will take good care of you." The older man left the room, a smile on his face.

"I can't believe it." PJ shook her head. "I woke up this morning with Charlie as my only family. Now I have a father, and a stepmother and brother when they find them and bring them home."

"Hey, don't forget me and my family."

"I saved the best for last." She cupped his cheeks and pulled his mouth close to hers. "I have a fantastic cowboy for a fiancé, and his wonderful family. Now shut up and kiss me like you mean it."

* * * * *

LARGER-PRINT BOOKS!
GET 2 FREE LARGER-PRINT NOVELS PLUS
2 FREE GIFTS!

◊ HARLEQUIN®

INTRIGUE®

BREATHTAKING ROMANTIC SUSPENSE

YES! Please send me 2 FREE LARGER-PRINT Harlequin Intrigue® novels and my 2 FREE gifts (gifts are worth about $10). After receiving them, if I don't wish to receive any more books, I can return the shipping statement marked "cancel." If I don't cancel, I will receive 6 brand-new novels every month and be billed just $5.49 per book in the U.S. or $5.99 per book in Canada. That's a saving of at least 13% off the cover price! It's quite a bargain! Shipping and handling is just 50¢ per book in the U.S. and 75¢ per book in Canada.* I understand that accepting the 2 free books and gifts places me under no obligation to buy anything. I can always return a shipment and cancel at any time. Even if I never buy another book, the two free books and gifts are mine to keep forever.

199/399 HDN F42Y

Name	(PLEASE PRINT)	
Address		Apt. #
City	State/Prov.	Zip/Postal Code

Signature (if under 18, a parent or guardian must sign)

Mail to the **Harlequin**® Reader Service:
IN U.S.A.: P.O. Box 1867, Buffalo, NY 14240-1867
IN CANADA: P.O. Box 609, Fort Erie, Ontario L2A 5X3

**Are you a subscriber to Harlequin Intrigue books
and want to receive the larger-print edition?
Call 1-800-873-8635 today or visit www.ReaderService.com.**

* Terms and prices subject to change without notice. Prices do not include applicable taxes. Sales tax applicable in N.Y. Canadian residents will be charged applicable taxes. Offer not valid in Quebec. This offer is limited to one order per household. Not valid for current subscribers to Harlequin Intrigue Larger-Print books. All orders subject to credit approval. Credit or debit balances in a customer's account(s) may be offset by any other outstanding balance owed by or to the customer. Please allow 4 to 6 weeks for delivery. Offer available while quantities last.

Your Privacy—The Harlequin® Reader Service is committed to protecting your privacy. Our Privacy Policy is available online at www.ReaderService.com or upon request from the Harlequin Reader Service.

We make a portion of our mailing list available to reputable third parties that offer products we believe may interest you. If you prefer that we not exchange your name with third parties, or if you wish to clarify or modify your communication preferences, please visit us at www.ReaderService.com/consumerschoice or write to us at Harlequin Reader Service Preference Service, P.O. Box 9062, Buffalo, NY 14269. Include your complete name and address.

HILP13R

REQUEST YOUR FREE BOOKS!

2 FREE NOVELS PLUS 2 FREE GIFTS!

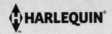

ROMANTIC suspense

Sparked by danger, fueled by passion

YES! Please send me 2 FREE Harlequin® Romantic Suspense novels and my 2 FREE gifts (gifts are worth about $10). After receiving them, if I don't wish to receive any more books, I can return the shipping statement marked "cancel." If I don't cancel, I will receive 4 brand-new novels every month and be billed just $4.74 per book in the U.S. or $5.24 per book in Canada. That's a savings of at least 14% off the cover price! It's quite a bargain! Shipping and handling is just 50¢ per book in the U.S. and 75¢ per book in Canada.* I understand that accepting the 2 free books and gifts places me under no obligation to buy anything. I can always return a shipment and cancel at any time. Even if I never buy another book, the two free books and gifts are mine to keep forever.

240/340 HDN F45N

Name _____ (PLEASE PRINT)

Address _____ Apt. #

City _____ State/Prov. _____ Zip/Postal Code

Signature (if under 18, a parent or guardian must sign)

Mail to the **Harlequin® Reader Service:**

IN U.S.A.: P.O. Box 1867, Buffalo, NY 14240-1867
IN CANADA: P.O. Box 609, Fort Erie, Ontario L2A 5X3

Want to try two free books from another line?
Call 1-800-873-8635 or visit www.ReaderService.com.

* Terms and prices subject to change without notice. Prices do not include applicable taxes. Sales tax applicable in N.Y. Canadian residents will be charged applicable taxes. Offer not valid in Quebec. This offer is limited to one order per household. Not valid for current subscribers to Harlequin Romantic Suspense books. All orders subject to credit approval. Credit or debit balances in a customer's account(s) may be offset by any other outstanding balance owed by or to the customer. Please allow 4 to 6 weeks for delivery. Offer available while quantities last.

Your Privacy—The Harlequin® Reader Service is committed to protecting your privacy. Our Privacy Policy is available online at www.ReaderService.com or upon request from the Harlequin Reader Service.

We make a portion of our mailing list available to reputable third parties that offer products we believe may interest you. If you prefer that we not exchange your name with third parties, or if you wish to clarify or modify your communication preferences, please visit us at www.ReaderService.com/consumerchoice or write to us at Harlequin Reader Service Preference Service, P.O. Box 9062, Buffalo, NY 14269. Include your complete name and address.
